FORGOTTEN FIRES

XOE MEYERS - BOOK FIVE

SARA C. ROETHLE

1

"So how does it feel to be a high school drop-out?" Chase asked as we both stared at the ceiling.

I squinted at the white plaster, then arched my back slightly, trying to find a more comfortable position on the carpet. "I just keep hearing every teacher and adult I've ever known telling me that high school drop-outs are destined to become life-long failures."

Chase turned his head and laid his cheek against the carpet so he could look at me. "You're going to get your GED. That's all I have."

I snorted as I let my head drop over to face him. "You're twenty-two and you don't even have a job."

Chase glared. "I work for your father. That's a job."

I laughed and turned my attention back up to the ceiling. "All you have to do is hang out with me. That is *not* a job."

"That's debatable," Chase replied. "Since we met I've been bitten by a vampire, held hostage in the lair of a psychotic, cannibalistic demon, and I killed my ex-girlfriend. Xoe, you are a lot of work."

I sighed. "At least I'm charming enough to make up for it all."

Chase laughed. "Also debatable."

My dad appeared in the doorway of Chase's room, causing us both to lift our heads from the carpet to look at him.

He looked down at me with green eyes the exact color of my own, and crossed his arms, wrinkling the corners of his pricey dress-shirt in his best responsible parent impression. "You should be studying, Xoe. You're going to take that test whether you like it or not."

I let my head fall back to the carpet with a soft thud. "I suffered through two and a half years of high school, only to come away with nothing. Let me mourn in peace."

"It was *your* choice to drop out," my dad replied, his words heavy with disapproval.

"I live in the demon underground, my mother barely speaks to me and doesn't want me in her house, my boyfriend has disappeared, and . . . I just can't go back there," I finished.

"You've still heard nothing from him then?" my dad asked, replacing his disapproval with sympathy.

My arms scratched across the carpet as I shrugged my shoulders on the ground. "Not since I forced him into a vehicle full of werewolves so he wouldn't get himself killed."

Chase moved his elbow across the ground to nudge my arm. "Jason loves you," he comforted, though there was a hitch in his voice as he said it. "He'll come back."

I closed my eyes and tried to turn off the strange feelings pulsing through my mind. I'd never been an anxious person, but in the past few months, I'd learned what true anxiety felt like. I took a deep breath and tried to think of a reply for Chase. Normally I'd be having such a conversation with Lucy and Allison, but with them busy with school and normal life, Chase and my dad had to be my stand-in girlfriends. They tried, but couldn't quite fit the bill.

I pictured Allison in my head. Given the chance, she would tell me to stop whining, and Lucy would be hard at work figuring out a solution to my problems. If the boys had taken some lessons from the girls, I probably wouldn't still be moping about on a bedroom floor of questionable cleanliness.

"You both need to get up and get out of this house," my dad announced.

With an exaggerated sigh, Chase stood, towering over my prostrate form at 6'1". He offered me a hand up, which I took grudgingly. We then stood looking at my dad, waiting for an explanation.

My dad rolled his eyes. "*Go.* I will not harbor slugs in my house."

"Gee dad, love you too," I quipped.

My dad stood aside and pointed a stern finger in the general direction of the front door.

Great. I'd already been kicked out of my mom's house, and now I was being kicked out of my dad's. At least in this situation I'd be allowed to come back . . . probably.

I followed Chase down the hall toward the front door, trailing my fingers along the freshly repainted walls as I went. A few weeks prior I had practically destroyed my dad's house by making a portal. My grandmother was the only other known demon with the skill, but she didn't leave destruction in her wake. I was strictly banned from portal making until we could figure out what I was doing wrong.

I'd destroyed my mom's house too, but my dad assured me that the damages had been repaired. I'd probably never get to see for myself if the house was okay. My throat tightened at the thought. I knew the events in my life were difficult for my loved ones to cope with, but I never thought I'd see the day when my mom couldn't bear to be near me. I knew she was just afraid, but that knowledge didn't make it any easier for me to deal with.

Chase helped me into my well-worn, brown leather jacket (a hand-me-down from Allison), to cover up the soft white tee shirt I was wearing, then put on his faded green, military style jacket. It would be cold outside because it was still snowy back in Shelby, and the demon underground tended to mirror the weather in the real

4

world. Still, a few months ago I would have been fine going out into the cold in my light-weight, hunter green tee shirt, but my demon hot-flashes had finally settled down.

I breathed in the cool air as we stepped outside and started walking. The exact mechanics of why it was currently cold in the underground still confused me, but I'd learned that the demon world was actually a parallel plane to the world of humans, like if the earth had a vast underground cave system filled with demons. Only, if you dug down in the real world, the demons wouldn't actually be there. You couldn't see humans from the underground, and humans couldn't see demons unless someone summoned one of us. The whole summoning thing was another confusing convention that I didn't quite understand.

Besides summoning, the only other way for full-blooded demons to see the human world was portals. Portals could allow full demons to travel above ground, or to any other realms for that matter, without all of the pesky drawbacks of summoning. Without portals, only those with a portion of human blood running through their veins could go to the human world, and even then only a few of them had the power to do so. My dad was one such demon. I, on the other hand, was currently stuck unless my dad sent me up, or I wanted to destroy his house again. We really needed to figure out the problem with my portals.

Chase grabbed my sleeve and pulled me aside as I nearly walked right into a mailbox. Yes, demons get mail too.

"Did you just venture off into Xoe land again?" Chase asked jokingly.

I'd been spacing out a lot lately. I couldn't help it. I had a lot on my mind.

"Where do you think Jason went?" I asked distantly for the billionth time.

Chase shrugged as we continued walking. "He's a big, scary vampire, Xoe. He can take care of himself."

I looked down at my sneakers as we walked. "I know. I just don't understand why he left. You'd think he could have at least written me a letter so I would know what's going on."

Chase sighed. We'd had this conversation many times before. "He'll come back."

I glanced over at Chase as we walked, feeling guilty for making him listen to my incessant whining about Jason, when he was probably the last person that wanted to hear it. He'd finally cut his black hair, and it was now short enough that you could barely tell how wavy it could be. My pale blonde hair fell limply past my shoulders, longer than I'd had it in years.

I wanted to ask Chase if he thought that Jason had somehow found out about our kiss, but I bit my tongue. I still didn't know what the kiss meant to me, and I was *so* not ready to talk about it with Chase. He'd let the whole thing go regardless. I'd been delirious with blood-loss, and he had saved my life. End of story.

We reached the steps of the large, gold-brick library and sat down side-by-side. The library's front steps had become our regular hangout since I'd been banished to the underworld. It was probably a strange place to choose, since we'd killed Chase's ex-girlfriend behind the building, but I liked it anyhow.

I leaned my shoulder against Chase's and watched the demons as they walked by. Most looked like normal humans, but there was the occasional red pair of eyes, or set of full-body scales mixed in with the crowd. No one paid us much mind, which was a comforting feeling in its own right. Sometimes it was nice to feel invisible.

My phone buzzed obnoxiously in my jacket pocket, disturbing the peaceful moment. It's strange, but I get perfect reception from most places in the underground. Maybe the demons had their own cell phone towers.

I checked my texts to see a new one from Allison. I almost ignored it, not feeling in the mood for talking, but went ahead and opened it. I could always just reply later.

The message read, "Hey Xoe, do you remember that girl Claire that was in our Biology class?"

I let out a huff of frustration, then replied facetiously, "Gee Allison, no hey, how are you doing? I know your mom disowned you and your boyfriend is missing, but what's important now is if you remember a girl named Claire."

I pushed send, then rolled my eyes at Chase as I waited for a reply.

My phone buzzed again and I looked down. "She's dead. She was murdered."

I paused for a few heartbeats, unsure of how to reply. I didn't actually remember who Claire was, and now I felt awful for not remembering.

The phone buzzed again. "This feels weird to me, Xoe. Too much has happened."

The reply was cryptic as best, but I understood. It probably wasn't wise to admit over text that we had been involved in a few . . . disappearances. Nothing had come back to bite us yet, but a part of me was always waiting for the other shoe to drop.

"I'll try to come up," I replied finally.

My phone buzzed again almost instantly. "Good. I'll be home."

Chase watched my expression, worry clear in his dark gray eyes. "What's going on, Xoe?"

I smiled weakly at him. "Sometimes I forget that you don't just read texts over my shoulder like Allison and Lucy do."

"Um, sorry for not reading your personal conversations?" he offered.

I stood. "A girl was killed in Shelby, and Allison has a bad feeling about it . . . but when we ask my dad to send us up we're just going to say that I want to see Allison and Lucy. Deal?"

"Maybe we shouldn't-" he began, but I had already started walking.

I really wasn't being arrogant in thinking that this girl's murder somehow involved me and my twisted little world. There was at least a fifty-fifty chance . . . no, make that sixty-forty . . . seventy-thirty? I shook my head as I walked. A demon's work is never done.

2
___

"Absolutely not," my dad said without even looking up at me.

He was sitting at what had replaced his little alchemy table. The new one had metal legs and a smooth glass tabletop, and looked horribly out of place with all the arcane-looking apparatus covering its shiny top. I had no idea what my dad was making, but it was probably just a special order from someone. He sold his concoctions in the underground for an insanely high price.

Dorrie was standing at his shoulder, handing him components without him having to ask. Her sparkly, white skin and long, translucent hair glistened as as the contents in the mortar went up in flame. She still wore the white jumpsuit I'd first met her in, though we'd convinced her to wash it a few times.

We were yet to figure out how to get Dorrie back to

the dream realm. She was a *driver*, sort of a golem made by demons, and was never supposed to leave the dream world to begin with. I had stolen her accidentally, though she didn't seem to blame me. I sighed as she watched my dad's work, her eyes sparkling in excitement. Yet another innocent person's life I had screwed up.

"Dad, you said you wouldn't harbor slugs," I argued. "I just want to see my friends."

"We could bring them down here?" he offered as he ground up what looked like a piece of coal in the basin of a little iron mortar.

"I'd love to meet Lucy, Dumpling," Dorrie chimed in happily, turning her brilliant blue eyes to me.

I offered Dorrie an apologetic smile. She'd met Allison during a brief visit, but could only meet Lucy if she came down, since Dorrie was confined to my dad's house. Given that she looked like she was made of ceramic and diamonds, Dorrie couldn't really blend in with a crowd. If the other demons found out she'd left the dream world, even unwillingly, she would be *unmade*. I wasn't sure what "un-making" entailed, but I knew I didn't want it to happen to Dorrie.

"We'll just be at Allison's house, I swear," I pleaded as I turned back to my dad.

When he didn't respond, I crossed my arms and began tapping my foot on the carpet until he put down what he was doing and faced me.

"*Why* won't you let me go?" I asked, my face hot with irritation.

His shoulders sagged as he sighed. "It's not safe."

I raised an eyebrow at him. "You'll let me wander around the demon underworld on my own, but the human world isn't safe?"

"It would be very difficult for Jason to get down here without demonic help," he replied in frustration, though his answer only served to add to my confusion.

"We want to *find* Jason," I replied a little shrilly, "not hide from him."

My dad looked at me like I was being stupid. "He disappeared for a reason, did he not? I'm not sure what happened between the two of you, but I'd venture to say that he's probably angry. Angry vampires can be dangerous."

"Jason would never hurt me," I answered, shocked by the implication. "And wait, why is *he* automatically the angry one? I could be the angry one, you know."

My dad smirked. "Of the latter I have little doubt, but you've known this vampire for a relatively short period of time. He could very well have just been behaving because he had you. Now without you, who knows?"

"*I* know," I stated firmly, pointing a finger at my chest. "I know Jason, and he would never hurt me."

My dad turned back to his work, and I almost thought the conversation was over when he asked, "Would you be able to hurt him to protect yourself or Chase?"

I paused for a moment as I considered his question. "I wouldn't let him hurt either of us, if that's what you're asking. Though he would never try in the first place."

My dad stood and put his hands on my arms, forcing me to give him my full attention. "Promise me, if you see him, you will be cautious."

"Yeah, yeah I promise," I mumbled as Chase came into the room. His timing alluded to the fact that he'd been eavesdropping out in the hall the entire time. So much for not snooping into my private conversations.

My dad let go of my arms and grabbed my hand, not looking terribly happy. I held out my free hand to Chase, who took it without a word. My dad's hand felt clammy in mine. If I didn't know any better I'd say he was nervous, but nervous about what? I had the sudden feeling of vertigo, then we were standing in front of Allison's house.

"I'll be back to get you in two hours," my dad said before disappearing in another puff of gray smoke.

I walked up the gravel driveway with Chase in tow to knock on Allison's bright purple front door. I looked up at the rest of the house while I waited, hoping that she was actually home and hadn't left because I took too long to come up. The house was three stories, rising far over our heads with its perfect white siding reflecting the sun. Growing up, the house had seemed like a mansion. Now it seemed somehow smaller. Funny how that happens.

The door swung inward to reveal Allison, looking tidy even though she was still wearing her red silk pajama set. Her normally long, honey-blonde hair now ended just above her shoulders.

"I think I have the wrong house," I joked as she posed, obviously wanting me to comment on her drastic haircut.

"Short hair is *in*," she explained before grabbing my hand and pulling me inside with a quick nod hello to Chase.

Everything in Allison's house is expensive looking, and I'd always felt slightly uncomfortable because of it. The familiar fear of breaking something that I couldn't in a million years pay to replace settled itself into the back on my mind as I glanced around at the creamy white walls and shiny, expensive furniture. The monstrous, flat-screen TV had been muted, but still played some show that seemed to be focused on food.

We went to sit on the cushy leather sofa in the middle of the room, leaving Chase to take the recliner. He didn't seem upset about the seating arrangement in the least as he pulled the lever on the side of the chair so he could lean back and close his eyes.

Realizing I had been watching Chase for longer than was normal, I turned to face Allison. "Now tell me about what happened to Claire," I pressed.

Allison tried to do her normal hair flip, but it fell short since her hair could no longer fall behind her shoulder. "Gee Xoe, no Allison how are you? Allison how have you been since I abandoned you and Lucy to finish high school without me?"

I eyed her patiently and waited for her to tell me about Claire.

"Well," Allison began conversationally, "her death was announced in class a few days ago, and I didn't think much of it. I know that sounds harsh, but we didn't really

know her, right? I just assumed it was a car crash or something, because no one really said any different. Then the
rumors started."

"As they always do," I encouraged. Chase still had his
eyes closed, but I knew he'd be listening intently. He
really didn't miss much.

"Claire was found in her bedroom by her little sister,
Rose. The sister had been kept home for a few days after
it happened, but when she was finally allowed to see her
friends she blabbed the whole thing. Claire's sister found
her lying in bed with blood all over her throat. It wasn't a
knife wound either. The skin was torn apart."

"Of course it was," I sighed. A cold knot was forming
in my stomach. Couldn't I ever get a break?

"It's just that after everything that happened with
Nick, and then with Maggie . . . " Allison let her words
trail of.

"I know," I replied somberly.

Nick had been a werewolf. I say *had been,* because my
dad killed him. He had worked with a group of witches
who kidnapped and killed supernaturals in an attempt to
steal their powers, but really they were all just puppets
for the demon Bartimus.

Maggie *had been* a vampire that tried to kill me. It
turned out she was also one of Bart's puppets. Bart had
been the one to kill her, though very few knew the actual
details, since Chase and I were the only ones present.

Even though I hadn't been the one to "pull the trig-
ger" on Maggie or Nick, they'd both still died for messing

with me. Enough time had passed that I was pretty sure no one would try to avenge Nick's death. The only people I could think of that would currently want revenge on me would be Maggie's sister, or Chase's ex-girlfriend Josie, and neither of them were around to get revenge on anyone anymore. I shuddered as I thought about the body-count. Most people get to go their entire lives without seeing a mangled corpse. I am not most people.

Josie's death had affected me a little more than the others, though I wasn't sure why. Maybe because I knew that she had been important to Chase at one point, and he was the one that had to kill her. We'd never really talked about it, even though I knew he mourned her death in his own way.

Many others had been hurt in Bart's attempts to get to me, but he was dead now too. This latest death couldn't have anything to do with him.

"Nick is dead," I stated. "Maggie and her sister are dead. Bart and Josie are dead. This can't have anything to do with us."

"There's one more thing," Allison said hesitantly.

I waited for her to continue, but she just curled up on the couch away from me and bit her lip.

"Tell me," I demanded.

She took in a deep, steadying breath. "I told Jason that you kissed Chase."

"You what!" Chase and I both exclaimed in unison. Chase was now sitting up, wide-eyed as he stared at Allison.

"I'm sorry!" she shouted back. "He came to see me after I went to talk to you about your mom wanting you to stay with your dad. He wanted to make sure you were alright, but he didn't want to see you."

I felt my heart skip a beat. "He didn't want to see me?" I questioned weakly.

It was a stupid question. If he had wanted to see me, he could have. Still, hearing someone else say it broke something inside of me.

Tears were flowing steadily down Allison's face. "He said he was going to leave for a while, give you time to sort things out, and then he would come back. I told him about Chase because I thought it would make him stay. I thought maybe making him aware of the competition would change his mind."

"But it didn't," I stated coldly. "I get it."

"No you don't, Xoe," Allison argued. "I've never seen Jason so angry. He scared me."

"So what?" I asked as my anger began to build. "You think he killed some random girl to get back at me?"

"No, I don't think that Xoe," she replied quickly. "I just thought I'd mention it, just in case."

"But you couldn't mention it to me as soon as you told him!" I shouted.

At some point I'd stood without realizing it, and suddenly Chase was standing too with his hand on my arm. "Let's take a walk," he said evenly.

He was right. It wasn't safe for me to be around Allison when I was angry, especially when my anger was directed at her in particular. I hadn't accidentally lit anything on fire recently, but it was still a possibility.

Chase led me slowly out of the house and we began walking down the road. It was cold enough that patches of snow could still be found amongst the trees, but there wasn't enough for the road to be icy. The underground might mirror the temperature of the human world, but the demons never got to see snow. The chilly Oregon air helped clear my head as my anger seeped away. Unfortunately my anger was soon replaced by tears.

"I'm sorry, Xoe," Chase said softly without looking at me. "This is all my fault."

I laughed, but it came out more like a sob. "Your fault? It's all *my* fault. I'm the one that pushed Jason away while I dealt with everything, and I'm the one that kissed you. I'm such an idiot."

Chase reached out and put a companionable arm around me as we walked. "It's going to be okay. We'll find Jason and we'll tell him what happened. You were delirious from blood loss when we kissed, and there was nothing else to it."

"It wasn't just blood loss," I mumbled, feeling a rush of anxiety at the admission.

I still wasn't ready to talk about things, but it looked like things were going to be talked about whether I wanted to or not. It wasn't fair just to keep it all to myself.

"You don't need to say that," Chase replied quietly.

The silence stretched out, with only the sound of our footsteps to keep us company. Chase still had his arm around me, and I took comfort in his presence. I felt guilty about that comfort, just as I felt guilty about everything else. I'd lied to Jason when I told him I didn't have any feelings for Chase, and I hadn't offered Chase any sort of explanation about my behavior. It wasn't fair.

I stopped walking and pulled away from Chase's arm so I could face him. "I kissed you because I have feelings for you. I think they've been developing for a while, but I also love Jason. I didn't know what to do about any of it, so I just didn't do anything. After this moment, I plan on continuing to do nothing until I can figure out a better course of action."

Chase raised his eyebrows in surprise. "That was probably one of the most honest statements I've ever heard."

I shrugged and looked down at the ground, embarrassed. "Get used to it. I have a lot of dishonesty to make up for."

"Dishonesty?" Chase questioned.

I shrugged again and continued to look down at the pavement. "Mostly to myself, I think, but some toward other people as well."

Chase nodded. "Are you ready to go back to Allison's now?"

"That's it?" I asked. "No comment on anything I just said?"

"I respect your decision to do nothing, and I respect your quest toward honesty," he replied, "but I'm not going anywhere regardless, so there's really nothing else for me to say."

I smiled weakly. "If only all things in life could be so simple."

Chase laughed. "Give me time," he joked. "I'm sure I'll figure out a way to complicate things."

We turned around and walked back toward Allison's house. Although not much had changed, a tremendous weight had been lifted off my chest. When I finally got to see Jason again, and I *would* get to see him, there would be nothing to lie about. Sure, there was a new murderer on the loose, and sure, I still had to study for my GED, but those things seemed far away from me.

A murderer may kill you, and homework may crush your mind, but a lie will eat at your soul until there's nothing left. I'd much rather deal with the murderer.

3

"I was only trying to help," were the first words out of Allison's mouth as she answered her front door.

"I know," I said apologetically. "It was all my own fault anyhow. I shouldn't have gotten mad at you."

"I really don't believe that Jason had anything to do with Claire's death," Allison added as we went back into her living room. "I guess I was just looking for some way to broach the subject. What I did seemed less terrible when compared to murder."

Allison and I sat back down on the couch, leaving Chase to stand awkwardly by the door. I looked back at him and gestured for him to sit, but he shook his head.

"I'm going to give you two some girl time," he announced as he rocked back and forth on his heels. "I think it's . . . needed."

He was right, but I still eyed him skeptically. "My dad will throw a fit if he finds out we split up."

Chase shrugged. "He'll survive." With that, he went back out the front door and closed it behind him.

Allison stared at the door for a few heartbeats, then turned back to me. "So what's the deal?" she asked excitedly. "Are you two dating now? Lucy will be totally bummed."

I inhaled to reply too quickly and ended up choking on my own spit. As I sputtered I managed to say, "Chill out. We're not together."

"So . . . you're still with Jason then?" she asked curiously.

"As you well know," I replied patiently, "I haven't spoken to Jason, but as far as I'm concerned we haven't broken up."

"Good," she replied. "Just checking."

"Why is that *good*?" I pressed.

Allison shrugged uncomfortably. "Just that I like Jason, and I know that he loves you, so you probably shouldn't trample all over his heart."

I almost wanted to cry at her blunt accusation. "He chose to leave even before he knew about the kiss," I said defensively. "I'm not the only one doing the trampling in this situation."

Allison raised her hands as if to ward off a blow. "I know, I know," she said soothingly. "It's just that you're so . . . tough. Sometimes it seems like other people might be more hurt by things than you are."

I glared at her. "Now that's the pot calling the kettle black."

Allison glared back. "What's that supposed to mean?"

Trying to keep my anger at a minimum, I replied, "You're the veritable ice queen of the group. Does that mean that you feel things less? No. It just means that you choose not to show them."

Allison snorted. "At least I just brush things off. *You* blow them up."

I narrowed my eyes at her. "Please tell me Lucy is on her way over."

I love Allison to death, but sometimes I needed a buffer. A few tense moments later my question was answered in the form of a knock on the door, and Lucy letting herself in before either of us could get up to answer.

With her werewolf speed Lucy was on me in an instant. Her hug nearly crushed my ribcage before she backed off with an apologetic blush.

She stood and looked back and forth between us. "Is there a reason for all of the tension currently in the room?"

"Just Xoe being Xoe," Allison replied.

"Just Allison being Allison," I mimicked.

Lucy sighed. "And now Lucy will be Lucy, and the two of you can love each other again."

Allison and I both smiled as Lucy stared us down, grudgingly at first, but within a few minutes we were all laughing.

"I can't believe this is the first time I've seen you since everything went down," Lucy chided as our laughter died down and she sat beside me, pushing her pin-straight, black hair behind her dainty ears.

She took off her blue wool coat as she adjusted to the temperature of the room, then straightened her white, button up shirt self-consciously. She was probably preparing for Allison to give her a hard time over her almost-matronly outfit, but Allison was too focused on watching my face to do so.

"My dad hasn't really wanted me to come up," I explained. "Plus, with not being able to go home, and being dropped out of high school . . . it just felt weird coming back."

"Well we're still here," Lucy consoled. "That hasn't changed. Also, are you guys aware that Chase is walking up and down the road by himself?"

I laughed. "He's giving us *girl time.*"

My smile was cut short as Allison scrutinized me for any reaction to the mention of Chase.

Lucy smirked, not noticing Allison's studious expression. "So are the two of you together now?"

I threw up my hands in exasperation. "*Why* does everyone keep asking me that?"

"Well Jason left . . . " Lucy replied softly.

"And he'll come back," I finished, needing to reassure myself more than anyone else.

Lucy shrugged. "I just wasn't sure that you would want to wait for him."

Allison gave me a knowing look. "And this is all coming from someone who doesn't even know that you kissed Chase."

That. That right there is why I needed an Allison buffer. Unfortunately my current buffer was looking a little sad about the news.

"I was delirious from blood loss," I began, but bit my tongue. No more lies. "And I *might* have some slight feelings for him."

Allison let out a sigh of relief. "At least you've finally admitted it."

"It wasn't *that* obvious," I snapped.

Allison laughed, not taking offense to my sour tone. "No, you're right. It was probably only obvious to those of us with *eyes*."

I pushed my back against the couch so I could sulk properly. "Can we please get back to talking about murder and other more lively subjects?"

Lucy nodded, not acknowledging my sarcasm. She still looked a little sad, and I hated it. While we were at a coalition meeting in Utah she had admitted to me that she had feelings for Chase. At the time I had done my best to assure her that I had no claim on him, legitimate or otherwise, and now here I was kissing him and trying to hide it from her.

Lucy gave me a scrutinizing look as if somehow sensing my thoughts, then explained, "I went to Claire's house today, well, not all the way to it, but near enough to sniff around."

"What are you, the local werewolf detective now?" I quipped.

Lucy rolled her eyes at me. "No, but I am a member of *your* werewolf pack, and we're supposed to keep an eye on things in our area."

Crap. I hadn't thought about that. While I'd been hiding out underground, I'd left Lucy, Max, and Lela alone to deal with any werewolf matters that might come up. In fact, I'd done that for most of my reign as pack leader so far.

I sighed. "Did you let Abel know about the murder?"

"I thought I'd leave that to you," Lucy said sweetly.

Abel was the leader of the werewolf coalition. He was the reason I was able to lead a werewolf pack in the first place, though I was still slightly skeptical about his motives. Regardless, he'd helped us out of a few sticky situations, and he'd sent other werewolves to keep my small pack safe while I was dealing with Bartimus. He might prove useful once again.

"Okay, okay," I held up my hands in a *don't shoot* gesture, "I'll call Abel. Just tell me what you found."

"I smelled vampire," Lucy stated blandly.

I held my breath while I waited for her to go on. Jason would never hurt anyone, especially not as some sort of weird revenge on me.

"Though I unfortunately can't really distinguish different vampire scents," she finished, taking in my worried expression, "not that I've met many vampires regardless. Wolves I can distinguish, but no wolf visited that house."

"So I call Abel and tell him there's a murderous vampire on the loose?" I questioned.

Lucy shrugged. "I smelled the vampire *near* Claire's house, that doesn't mean that he or she was the one to commit murder. It could just be a coincidence."

That was Lucy, ever reasonable.

"But her throat was torn apart," Allison argued. "I'd say that pretty clearly points to a vampire."

"Or someone wanting the murder to *look* like it was done by a vampire," I suggested.

Allison snorted. "And who would go to the trouble? I'm sure the police are thinking *human*, so why make it look like anything else?"

I shook my head. If Jason had been around, he would have told me that it wasn't my business. I was already involved in enough trouble, and I didn't need to go searching for more . . . but Jason wasn't around, and there was a chance that this murder could be some sort of message for my little werewolf pack. It was time to do some digging. Hey, a girl's gotta have a hobby.

I excused myself to the kitchen to call Abel. Though I'd spoken to him countless times, I still felt nervous about calling him. I glanced down at the bracelet on my wrist as I searched for Abel's number in my cell phone. The ugly piece of jewelry, if you could call something made of intricately woven, blue twine jewelry, was a gift from Abel, and I'm using the term *gift* very loosely here.

The bracelet basically said that Abel *owned* me, to put it quite crudely. What it really meant was that he had my back. If anyone messed with me, it meant they were messing with him. Since he was the head of the Werewolf Coalition, it pretty much meant that they were messing with all of the werewolf packs of the Western United States, and a bit of Canada. I still didn't trust Abel's intentions in giving me the bracelet, and it was yet to prove useful, but I'd feel pretty silly if I got into trouble and didn't have the bracelet to use as leverage.

Next to the ugly, blue bracelet was a dainty charm bracelet. The only charms on it were a heart, and a small, golden serpent with little red eyes. The heart was a gift from Brian, a friend that didn't really want to be my friend anymore, but the serpent had been a Christmas present from Chase. The bracelet had spent a lot of time in my jewelry box. I had told myself it was for safe keeping, but really I just wasn't sure if Jason would be offended by me wearing jewelry from two different boys. Okay, I was worried that he wouldn't like the gift from Chase. I had just recently started wearing it again, and I felt silly for not wearing it all along since I actually really liked it.

On that same hand was the ring my dad had given me. It had a red stone that occasionally emitted flashing, swirling lights. It had originally been my grandmother's. The ring I did *not* like, but my dad insisted I wear it for some reason.

I found Abel's number and pushed the send button.

After several rings my anxiety eased. Maybe he wouldn't pick up.

"Hello?" a jovial voice answered . . . a jovial voice that did not belong to Abel.

"Of course you would be the one to answer," I grumbled.

"And how are you, Xoe?" Devin's voice replied sarcastically.

Devin was Abel's number two, and that was most of what I knew about him. I also knew that I didn't trust him. Devin struck me as the type of man that was only out to serve his own purposes. I was pretty sure the only reason he'd supported me becoming a pack leader was because he'd placed bets on the situation. The odds were not in my favor, and he'd won a good chunk of money.

"Put your almighty leader on the phone, please," I replied, ignoring his question.

Devin snorted. "The almighty one is unavailable at the moment."

"Is it his nap time?" I joked grumpily.

"You know how cranky he gets without it," Devin replied. "I assume you're calling about the murder in your area?" he added.

I was so surprised that I couldn't think of a witty reply, and instead just stood with my jaw agape and the phone pressed to my ear. I heard the front door open and close in the other room, but couldn't focus on it as I tried to think of what to say to Devin.

"I'll take that silence as a yes?" Devin prompted.

"You people really do know everything, don't you?" I said finally.

Devin laughed. "What kind of werewolf secret society would we be, if we didn't stay well informed?"

I took a deep breath. "Well I guess I didn't need to call after all."

Chase came into the kitchen behind me, then seeing that I was still on the phone, took a seat at one of the stools at the kitchen counter.

"Not really," Devin replied. "I'll be seeing you soon enough."

I almost dropped the phone in surprise, then fumbled it back up to my ear. "Come again?" I asked, hoping I'd misunderstood.

"My flight leaves in a few hours," he explained. "I don't imagine you'd like to pick me up from the airport?"

I shook my head even though Devin obviously couldn't see it. "Why are you coming? I highly doubt you normally investigate every murder that comes along."

"Not every murder," he said happily, "but one in the hometown of our favorite little demon? I wouldn't miss it for the world."

"I don't have a car to pick you up in," I replied, giving in to the inevitable. "Take a cab."

Devin sighed loud enough that I could hear it clearly over the phone. "Can you at least promise that you won't be hiding out in demon-land when I get there?"

"How did you . . . " I trailed off, not liking the fact that he already knew I'd been hiding out in the demon underground.

"What kind of werewolf secret society would we be, if-" he began.

"I get it," I snapped cutting him off. I rattled off Allison's address, then added, "I'll try to be here, but I make no promises."

Devin sighed again. "I'll call you when I arrive."

With that, he hung up. I pulled the phone away from my ear with an angry huff and turned my attention to Chase.

"Is Abel coming?" he asked.

"Devin," I groaned. "And he wants us to be here to meet him."

Chase snorted. "Good luck with that. I'm sure your dad will be here any time now to pick us up."

"Why is he so worried?" I asked, frustrated.

Chase rolled his eyes and stood. "You've almost died several times on your dad's watch. I don't blame him for being a little paranoid, and I'd be lying if I said I wasn't worried too."

I crossed my arms and glared up at him. "And why on earth are *you* worried?"

"Why on earth are you not?" he countered. "A girl your age, in your town, gets murdered in her bed, and it looks like a vampire kill."

"So you think it has something to do with me?" I asked, even though I agreed with him.

Chase shrugged. "I'd say that the chances of it being a

coincidence are very, *very* slim. Even if it isn't a direct message for you, it might be some sort of challenge to your pack."

I leaned my back against the wall to brace myself for what was coming. "Is this where you tell me that I need to run and hide?"

Chase gave me a look like I was being silly. "No, this is where I tell you that *we* need to get to the bottom of this. We can't just sit around and wait for things to get worse."

I grinned, though I felt shaky with nerves. "Are you saying you'll be the Watson to my Holmes?"

Chase laughed, easing some of the tension. "Only if I get to wear a cape."

Allison walked into the kitchen, followed by Lucy. "I'd say we've got more of a *Scooby Doo* thing going on," Allison commented as she took Chase's vacated stool.

Lucy crossed her arms and glared at Allison. "You better not be implying that I'm Scooby."

Allison shrugged. "You *do* have a tendency to turn furry."

Ignoring Allison, Lucy turned to look up at me. "When does Devin arrive?"

I would never get used to werewolf hearing. "He said his flight leaves in a few hours, but I didn't think to ask for an exact time."

"So you'll stay here this evening then?" Allison asked, not stating that if I was remaining above ground, I really didn't have anywhere else to go.

I shrugged, feeling morose at the reminder of my

mom not wanting to see me. "I have to talk to my dad first. It was difficult enough to get him to bring us up to begin with."

Allison snorted. "Like you're any safer in the demon underground? You've almost died there on multiple occasions."

I shook my head. "Don't ask."

I lifted my cell phone once again to call my dad, then walked back into the living room for a little privacy. Lucy would hear everything that was said regardless, but at least I had the *illusion* of privacy.

He answered on the first ring. "Alexondra, I was just about to call you."

"Maybe I'm developing psychic powers," I joked.

"What?" he questioned. "Oh, you're joking," he went on before I could clarify. "What were you calling about?"

He sounded nervous, and I didn't like it one bit. "What aren't you telling me?" I pressed.

"Nothing," he said a little too quickly. "I have quite a bit of work to do here, so I was just thinking that perhaps you and Chase could stay with your friends tonight."

My eyes widened in surprise. Here I'd thought I had a huge argument ahead of me. "You know, most parents don't encourage coed sleepovers."

My dad laughed, but it was strained. "Oh please, like anything would ever happen between you and Chase."

"What is that supposed to mean?" I asked, slightly offended.

"He's five years older than you," he replied like it was

obvious. "You can't date someone five years older than you."

I snorted. "Uh, Jason is like a hundred years older than me."

My dad was silent for a moment. "You know, I hadn't really thought about it like that," he answered finally. "You haven't already started dating Chase, have you?"

He'd asked the question in a joking way, but I could tell he actually wanted an answer. It was the question of the day, apparently. "No," I answered simply.

"And you don't plan on it?"

I could feel a nervous blush creeping up my neck. If one more person questioned me about Chase, I was going to scream. "No," I answered again.

"What was that hesitation?" he asked suspiciously.

"There was no hesitation!" I shouted. "I'll see you tomorrow."

"Xoe!" he shouted before I could hang up.

I took a deep breath. "Yes?"

"You'll just be staying at Allison's like you promised, right?"

"Ye-es," I said tiredly, drawing the word out for emphasis.

I could almost hear my dad nodding to himself. "Be careful," he said finally.

"I will," I replied, just before the phone went dead. My dad wasn't telling me something, but I didn't have time to think about it as Chase walked into the room.

"Lucy and Allison are ordering pizza," he began until

he saw the look on my face. "What's wrong? What happened?"

I shoved my phone angrily into my jeans' pocket. "Nothing," I mumbled. "Hey Lucy!" I shouted, though I didn't really need to shout for her to hear me.

She came into the living room, phone in hand.

"Don't order yet," I explained. "Let's go out."

Lucy nodded and turned to go back into the kitchen. Chase looked at me like I'd lost my mind, but I hadn't. I'd simply chosen to focus on the task at hand. The first step to solving any crime is digging for gossip, and we weren't going to hear anything of the sort shut up in Allison's house.

Shelby's local pizza place, Irvine's, was also Shelby's only pizza place. It was therefore always filled with teenagers. In other words, gossip central. Maybe my teenage high school life wasn't over after all. It was a mixed blessing, at best.

4

After Allison got dressed, we all piled into her car. It was lucky that Allison had a car, as both Lucy and I were car-less, and Chase had sold his old, beat up truck for parts once it stopped running for the final time.

I sat in the front next to Allison, leaving Chase and Lucy in the back. We were going to pick up Max on the way, but our pack would be incomplete, as Lela had to work. I had a nervous knot in my stomach as we drove. The streets and buildings of Shelby looked somehow different to me. It was like everything was smaller, making me feel almost claustrophobic despite the open expanses of forest.

The thought of going into Irvine's made me more nervous still. I'd probably see people that I knew, and if I wanted to find out more gossip about Claire's death, I would have to talk to them. The questions about dropping out would be inevitable, and I wouldn't quite know how to answer them. *Yeah, see, the thing is, I'm a demon, and other monsters keep trying to kill me, so public high school just isn't right for me at this point in my life.*

I was startled as Allison pulled onto a gravel driveway and shut off the car. Had we reached Max's already? I really hadn't thought about how being back in Shelby would affect me, but I felt dazed and a little traumatized.

Max emerged from the front door of his small, modular home and approached Allison's car. Without a word, Lucy slid to the middle seat, making room for Max to sit behind Allison. Max got into the car, then we were moving once again.

As we pulled back onto the main road, Max reached across Lucy to pat my shoulder. "You're looking a little pale there, packmaster."

"Mind your own business, minion," I joked back, but my heart wasn't in it. At that moment, I just wanted to be back in the underground, safe in my dad's house. I shook my head. What was wrong with me? The ride to Irvine's was over in a flash, and before I knew it we came to a stop once again.

Max exited the car on Allison's side, saying something to her that I didn't quite catch. Allison laughed, then leaned down slightly to *kiss* Max hello.

I stood on the other side of the car watching them, completely stunned. The last time I'd talked to Max about Allison, she was annoyed with him because he wouldn't make her a werewolf.

SARA C. ROETHLE

"Did I miss something?" I blurted as I walked around the car to approach them.

Allison turned to smirk at me, not flustered as she predicted my reaction. "You *knew* we had gone on a few dates."

I let out a huff of disbelief. "Yeah, but you were just trying to trick him into making you a werewolf."

Max glared at me. "So the only reason Allison would ever choose to date me is because I'm a werewolf?"

I glared back. "*You* told me that was the reason she dated you, and the dating ended when you refused to turn her. What else was I supposed to think?"

Max still looked cranky, but gave a curt nod in assent. "Well we've worked out our differences. Get over it."

I threw my hands up and turned away. "Whatever!" I exclaimed. "We've got bigger problems."

Max mumbled something I couldn't quite hear, and Allison shushed him. It was better that I didn't hear, as my control over my temper was tenuous at best. Stress made my anger more difficult to control, and I'd had about all of the stress I could deal with for one lifetime.

Max sped up to walk next to Chase, as Lucy and Allison fell behind to walk on either side of me.

"What's wrong?" Lucy asked as she looked up at me nervously, shielding her dark, almond-shaped eyes from the sun with her hand.

"You can't be this upset about Max and I," Allison added before I could answer.

I shook my head and looked forward, feeling embar-

38

rassed for snapping at Max and Allison, given my nerves had nothing to do with them.

"I'm sorry Al, I just didn't realize how weird it would feel to be back here," I explained. "It seems like it was years ago that we met Jason, but it hasn't even been a full year."

Lucy stopped walking and smiled bitterly. "I know what you mean. Normal life seems like a distant dream."

"A *bad* dream," Allison cut in, purposefully bumping into my shoulder to make me bump into Lucy. "You guys can't tell me that you haven't enjoyed all of the excitement, at least a little."

"Oh yes. Allison," I said sarcastically as I turned to face her. "Almost being killed every month is great fun."

Allison rolled her honey-colored eyes. "You know what I mean. We get to know this big secret, and be a part of things that other teenagers will never be a part of. It's *cool*."

I snorted. "Destroy your mom's house, help kill your friend's girlfriend, and lose track of your vampire boyfriend, *then* tell me how cool it all is."

"Oh you're such a party pooper," Allison chided, though she grabbed my hand and gave it a reassuring squeeze to soften her words.

"Are you guys coming or what?" Max called out as he and Chase waited near the door to the pizza parlor. They looked an odd pair, with Chase standing at 6'2" and Max barely reaching 5'4", just like Allison and Max looked an odd pair. Of course, I was a half-demon with a vampire boyfriend. Who was I to judge odd pairs?

We started walking again and quickly reached the boys. Max held the door open for us as we entered the loud, crowded interior, and I realized with a start that is was Saturday. I'd lost track of the days being in the underground. As we walked through the crowd I saw several people I knew. Instead of waving or saying hi, they all gave me strange glances liked they wondered what I was doing there.

"Why is everyone staring at me?" I whispered to Lucy as we waited for a group of departing people to get out of our way.

Lucy cringed. "There may be a few rumors going around school about you."

The group that was blocking us finally left so we could be seated. Most of the tables were filled, and we ended up with a booth that was yet to be cleared of the dirty plates and empty pizza pan from its previous patrons. Lucy, Allison and I squeezed into one side, squeaking across the red vinyl fabric of the booth as we all tried to fit. Meanwhile Chase and Max sat comfortably on the other side. We all waited silently as one of the waitresses approached to clean our table.

As the waitress walked away, I turned to look at Lucy. "*What* rumors?"

Lucy shrugged uncomfortably. "Well you kind of just disappeared, and so did Jason. No one really knew Jason, but they'd seen you together around town."

"And?" I prompted when she didn't continue.

"Everyone thinks that you and Jason eloped and ran off together," Max finished explaining for her.

I dropped my head into my palms and groaned. Couldn't they have thought of a more creative explanation?

"I'm seventeen," I mumbled through my hands.

"Your mom could have given consent," Allison explained.

The waitress came back to take our order while my face remained buried in my palms. I suppose being married wasn't the worst rumor in the world, but I still didn't like it. I looked up as the waitress left, just in time to see something catch Max's eye.

His mouth fell open in surprise as he turned slowly to look at me. "Don't look now, but your husband is sitting at that booth over there."

I turned around so quickly that I nearly shoved Allison out of her seat. Sure enough, Jason was sitting at a booth across the restaurant from ours. He sat with two other people, all leaned in having what looked like an intense conversation. I didn't recognize his company. One was a man with closely cropped blonde hair and a tall, thin frame. The other was a woman with black hair that fell just past her chin. I couldn't make out many other details with the distance and people walking in between us, but the pair appeared to be in their mid-thirties.

When I recovered enough to think, I made a shooing gesture to get Allison out of my way. Once I was free from the booth, I made my way across the chaotic restaurant toward Jason's table, leaving my friends to sit silently in my wake.

Jason noticed me when I was halfway across the room, and his eyes widened in surprise. If I didn't know any better, I'd say he looked almost scared. He quickly excused himself from his companions and stood to meet me before I could reach them.

"Let's go outside," he said as soon as we stood facing each other.

I looked him up and down, taking in his moderately dressed-up appearance. He wore all black, and his hair was actually combed as opposed to it's usual, tousled mess.

When I just stood there staring at him, he grabbed my arm and guided me toward the door. I looked back to my friends for reassurance, but from the angle the only two I could see were Max and Chase. Max looked nervous, and Chase looked ready to jump up and follow us out of the restaurant.

Jason dropped my arm to open the door, and suddenly we were alone in the chilly outside air. I turned angry, hurt eyes up at him as we walked a little further away from the restaurant. I had told myself that once I finally found Jason, I'd play it cool, but as I looked up at his stony expression, I knew there was no way I'd achieve that particular goal.

Jason stopped near Allison's car and turned slowly to

face me. "I thought you were staying underground," he said blandly as his dark blue eyes met mine.

My pulse sped. "Really?" I asked breathlessly. "After everything that happened, you just left, and that's all you have to say to me?"

Jason clenched and unclenched his fists a few times, making me remember Allison's earlier comments about his anger, but his face remained calm. "I just need some time, Xoe, and I think you do too."

"Don't tell me what I need!" I shouted. A couple walking nearby turned and gave me uncomfortable looks before getting into their car.

"Fine," Jason conceded, drawing my gaze back to his face. "*I* need time. I'm sorry."

I shook my head and pinched the bridge of my nose to stave off the dull throb of a building headache. "Normally, when you want to take a break from someone, you *tell* them," I said tiredly, not looking up to meet his gaze.

He wrapped his arms tightly around himself, symbolically putting distance between us. "I told Allison," he explained. "I knew if I told you directly, you would get upset. I don't think I would have been able to stay away if you asked me not to."

I took a deep breath and tried to slow the beating of my heart. It wouldn't help anything if I accidentally blew up someone's car. "I know we had a fight before you left," I explained calmly, "but it was just a fight. I assumed we would talk and everything would be okay."

"It wasn't just a fight," he argued, finally dropping his

arms to his sides. "All I've ever tried to do is keep you safe, but you don't listen to a word I say."

"You were asking me to hide when my dad and Chase were in danger!" I exclaimed. "I'm sorry I couldn't do what you wanted, but they could have *died*."

"And you could have died!" he yelled back, finally showing some emotion. "You've come so close to death so many times, and you act like none of it bothers you. It's selfish to endanger yourself when there are people who care about you."

I bit my lip to keep from screaming at him. When I felt calm enough to speak, I said, "Selfish? You're honestly going to tell me that helping my friends form a werewolf pack, and not wanting anyone I care about to die is *selfish*?"

Jason sighed. "I know you have the best intentions, Xoe, but you're not looking at the bigger picture. In going to Utah to form a pack for Lucy and Max, you forced Chase and I into a dangerous situation too. By getting involved in the werewolf community, you've put your mother in danger. You destroyed her home and basically destroyed her life. If I had been able, I would have followed you into the underground when you went after Josie, and it kills me that I wasn't there to protect you."

I shook my head as tears began to build behind my eyes. "You act like I had a choice in all of this," I muttered as I began to cry. "Why is it okay for you to protect me, but it's not okay for me to protect everyone else?"

Jason looked away from my tears. "There is always a choice," he mumbled.

"And *you* chose to leave," I accused, suddenly angry again. "I may have hurt my mom, but she completely bailed on me. Do you know how it feels to be shut out by your own mother? And you just left me to deal with it alone. I *needed* you."

"You had your dad and Chase, and Lucy *and* Allison. You weren't alone," Jason replied bitterly. "You know *nothing* about being completely alone."

He was right, but it still stung that he wasn't there. "Having friends around is not the same as having a partner. *You* were supposed to be there for me?"

"And they're all just *friends*?" he asked bitterly.

I suddenly remembered that Jason knew I had kissed Chase, and here I'd just been yelling at him about how horrible *he* was. "About Chase," I began.

"Allison told me," he cut me off. "It's not why I left."

"I-I know," I stammered. "I just wanted you to hear it from me."

Jason was silent for a moment, then seemed to release some of his tension with a sigh. "Was it only the one time?" he asked finally.

I nodded.

"I need to go," Jason stated, surprising me with his bluntness.

"What?" I asked, confused. "No yelling? You're not even upset?"

SARA C. ROETHLE

"It was just a kiss, Xoe," he said like I was being child-ish. "We have bigger problems to deal with."

He could play things down all he wanted, but I'd heard the anger in his voice just moments before. "Well you leaving isn't what I'd call *dealing* with things," I replied quickly.

Jason sighed and looked back at Irvine's. I'd almost forgotten that we'd both come with other people. "What are you doing above ground?" he asked as he gazed off into the distance.

"What, am I not allowed to be here?" I snapped, then bit my lip. Getting angry again would get me nowhere.

"You haven't come up since you left that day," he explained as he turned his gaze back to me, not reacting to my tone.

"How do you know?" I asked suspiciously. "You told Allison you were *leaving*."

Jason glared at me. "Well I didn't go far," he admitted, "but you never answered my question."

I wanted to say I was just up to visit Lucy and Allison, but I stopped myself. No more lies. "A girl was killed," I explained.

Jason nodded. "I know. Her parents hired me to find out who did it."

It took me a moment to close my gaping jaw. "Why on earth would her parents hire *you*?"

Jason gave me a confused look. "You don't know?"

"No . . . " I trailed off, hoping for an explanation.

"Her parents are witches," Jason explained, "and so

46

was Claire. The human police are out of their depth on this one."

I had a tendency to forget that Jason was a bounty hunter by trade. He hadn't worked much since we'd gotten together. There hadn't been much time.

"Devin is on his way to Shelby," I offered, seeing as Jason had been honest with me. "Abel was worried that the murder had something to do with my pack, but maybe he was wrong. I don't think he knows that Claire was a witch."

Jason looked at me curiously. "Does this mean that you will back off and not get involved in things for once?"

I opened my mouth, then closed it. If Claire was killed because she was a witch, I really might not need to get involved. Yet, there was no way to be sure.

"No," I answered simply.

Jason threw his hands up in exasperation. "Why *not*?" he snapped.

"Witches were killed before when Bart was trying to get to me. I can't just write off Claire's death and hope for the best," I explained.

"I'm being paid to figure out who did this," he replied. "Please just wait until I find something out before you come running in."

Movement in my peripheral vision caught my eye. I turned to see the two people Jason had been meeting with walking toward us. "Who are they?" I whispered before they could reach us.

47

"More witches," he said at a normal volume. "I have to go."

I grabbed his arm before he could walk away. "We still need to talk about us," I pleaded.

Jason nodded as he pulled away from me. "Just back off from this case. I'll contact you when I know something, and we can talk about everything else as well."

I let him walk away then. Rather than going back into Irvine's, Jason and the two witches got into a silver SUV and drove away. I stood in the parking lot and watched them go, feeling an odd mixture of emotions. I probably should have gone back into Irvine's, but I couldn't seem to move my feet.

Eventually Allison and Lucy came out to the parking lot to check on me. Allison put her arm around my shoulders as she reached my side. "You've been standing alone in this parking lot for a mighty long time," she observed.

"We didn't figure anything out, and he just left," I replied, feeling stunned as I reflected on our conversation.

"And you just let him leave?" Lucy asked from my other side.

I shook my head. "He asked me to leave Claire's death alone, and he'd find me when he had more information."

"What a jerk," Allison grumbled.

"He's not a jerk," I said quickly. "He's right. He was right about everything, but I just can't help it."

"Help what?" Lucy asked, confused.

I shook my head. "I just can't help getting involved. I

can't sit back and let Jason investigate Claire's murder. If it has something to do with me, then I need to know."

"We're not going to argue with you on that," Allison replied. "Though if Jason is working on it too, we should all be working together. Explain to me again *why* Jason is working on it?"

"Claire was a witch," I answered. "Her parents hired him."

"You really should have led with that information," Lucy chided.

I looked past Allison to see Max and Chase emerging from Irvine's with several boxes of pizza in hand. At my questioning look, Allison explained, "We talked to everyone we could while you were with Jason. They all know the story that Claire's sister blabbed, but that's about it. We figured we'd eat at my place instead."

I nodded in understanding, glad I didn't have to go back into Irvine's, and suspecting that Lucy and Allison knew just how badly I didn't want to go back inside.

When the boys reached us, we all piled back into Allison's car. The smell of pizza permeated the interior, making me feel hungry and sick at the same time. I wasn't sure if my nervous stomach would even let me eat once we got to Allison's. You knew it was a bad day when Alexondra Meyers would turn down a slice of pizza.

5

We pulled into Allison's driveway to find my dad already waiting for us. He checked his shiny, silver watch that went with his designer charcoal suit as Allison brought the car to a stop.

"What happened to just staying here?" he asked with a scowl as I got out of the car.

I glared at him. "We got hungry."

He waited while everyone else got out of the car and went for Allison's front door. I tried to follow them inside, but he caught me by the arm and held me back. "I need to talk to you in private, Alexondra."

My friends all hustled inside, shutting the door behind them. Traitors.

"When does Devin arrive?" he asked as soon as we were alone.

"How did you . . . " I began, but then I realized just how he knew. "You talked to Abel, didn't you?"

"I knew you were up to something," he replied, as if it justified him going behind my back to ask Abel what was going on.

I clenched my jaw in annoyance, but kept my inner tirade to myself. "Tonight," I answered sharply. "He didn't give me an exact time."

"And you plan on investigating this murder?" he asked casually.

Suspicious at his tone, I looked up at his expression. His earlier annoyance had disappeared as if it had never existed to begin with.

"Yes?" I said like it was a question.

"Well then you'll want to meet with the local coven," he stated just as casually. "They would know if anyone had anything against Claire's family."

I crossed my arms and peered up at him. "You're really not going to drag me home kicking and screaming?"

My dad sighed, and suddenly looked tired. "You're seventeen, and you're smart. I can't very well go around making rules for a daughter I wasn't even around to raise."

"Well up until today, you've been doing just that," I countered. "What changed?"

He shifted from foot to foot, as if uncomfortable with the conversation. "Every situation you've gotten yourself into, you've also gotten yourself out of," he explained. "All you want to do is take care of your friends, just as I've failed at taking care of you. Being raised around humans obviously did you good, and I won't stop you from being a better person than I am, than most demons are, for that matter."

I wasn't expecting such a heartfelt admission, and it left me at a loss for words. I also wanted to point out that he was the one to get me out of several of the more sticky situations, but I figured I'd keep my mouth shut while I was ahead.

My dad gave me an awkward pat on the shoulder. "I brought some of your things," he went on, "and I set up a meeting with the local coven. They refuse to meet with me, but they've agreed to meet with you ... and Devin."

This was just way too easy. "Is it really a good idea for me to meet with witches? The only other witches I've met were trying to kill me."

My dad shrugged. "They're human, and you'll have werewolf backup. Plus, you're trying to help them. While the majority of witches are organized, they're nothing like the werewolves. They will receive little help outside of their individual coven."

I nodded, still trying to get over the fact that not only was my dad letting me stay, he was helping me. "Well, thanks for the tips?" I offered, not sure of what else to say.

"I just want you to promise me one thing," he said quickly before I could try to walk away.

I took in a deep breath and prepared myself for the lecture that I had expected initially.

"It's okay for you to protect your friends," he began, "but don't forget about yourself."

"I'll be careful," I said tiredly.

"That's not what I mean," he replied. "Don't forget about yourself as a person. Both your grandmother and I forgot, and now we're both alone. If you focus too much on every emergency that comes along, you'll lose yourself in the process. Think about what makes you happy, and make sure that you don't lose it."

Finally he stopped talking, which was good, because I was beginning to feel incredibly awkward. I was used to having heart-to-hearts with my mom, but I'd never really expected to have one with my dad.

"Do you promise?" he said when I offered no reply.

"Y-yeah," I stammered. "I promise."

With that, he handed me a small piece of paper and disappeared in a puff of smoke. I looked down at the paper to find an address I didn't recognize, and the word "midnight". The witches wanted to meet at midnight. How portentous.

I wrapped my arms around myself and thought about what my dad had said. *Think about what makes you happy.* I hadn't really thought about that in a long time. I thought about keeping everyone alive, and about doing my best to keep *them* happy, but I hadn't really considered myself. Mostly I'd just thought that if the people I cared about were alive and well, then that was good enough.

I shook my head and went for the front door. I'd think about it another time. For now I'd just worry about meeting with a coven of witches. I went inside to discover that everyone had retired to the kitchen to eat. Two small suitcases were sitting by the inside of the door. Apparently my dad had popped right in when he'd discovered that no one was home.

I went into the kitchen to find everyone sitting at the dining table with all of the pizza boxes open, and parmesan and red pepper strewn about. I took the empty seat next to Chase with Lucy sitting further left, then Max further left still, and Allison at the corner on my right. I was somewhat relieved that Allison and Max weren't sitting together. I really didn't mind them dating, but I could only take so much change at once. Before grabbing a slice of pepperoni, I handed Chase the little piece of paper that my dad had given me.

He looked it over, then looked up at me in confusion. "Am I supposed to know what this means?"

"Devin and I are going to meet the local witches tonight," I explained.

"So he's really letting you stay?" he asked, confused. "I mean, I saw the suitcases, but I really did not see this coming."

I shrugged as I bit into my pizza, feeling instantly better as the cheesy bite slid down my throat. "Something weird is going on with him," I replied thoughtfully. "He got all . . . sentimental on me. I feel like he's hiding something."

"Hmmf," Chase replied with a thoughtful expression on his face.

"Why only you and Devin?" Lucy asked from Chase's other side. "Doesn't he remember what happened the last time we ran into a group of witches?"

I shrugged. "He doesn't seem to think it will be a problem, and I'm guessing the witches don't want to host an entire werewolf pack, especially since one of them was recently murdered."

"We should at least come and wait in the car," Lucy argued. "Just in case."

I nodded and took another bite of my rapidly cooling pizza. "Agreed. Despite the fact that my dad seems to trust them, or he's at least not afraid of them, I really don't want to end up in the back of a van getting injected with tranquilizers again. That was just no fun."

Lucy smiled. "Yes, let's avoid all badly lit dungeons while we're at it."

Allison, who had been silent until then, finally perked up. "Do you guys think this could have something to do with what happened before?"

The *before* we were all referring to was the time we were all kidnapped by witches and a werewolf who were trying to steal other people's powers. It was all a scheme set up by the demon Bartimus, and Bart was dead. I'd personally witnessed my grandmother removing his head from his body.

"It wouldn't make any sense," I replied. "Even if the few survivors were still trying to achieve their goal, they'd have nothing to gain from killing another witch."

"We'll know more after you meet with the coven," Chase assured. "Until then, try not to over-think it."

I sighed. Asking me to not over-think things was like asking a fish to stop swimming. In an attempt to distract myself, I rose from my seat and pulled out my phone, then walked into the living room to call Lela. Done eating, Allison and Max followed me, then sat on the couch to watch TV. Irritated by the extra noise, I stepped out the front door to make my call. Lela answered on the second ring. Yes, she would come with to meet the witches, yes, she would be over in just a few minutes. With that settled, I went back inside. Averting my eyes from the spectacle of Allison and Max snuggling up on the love seat, I went back into the kitchen.

Lucy and Chase both stopped talking as soon as they saw me. I gave them a suspicious look as I put my phone back in my pocket.

"Why do I feel like my ears should be burning?" I asked as I crossed my arms across my chest.

"No reason," Chase answered quickly as he looked up at me with a big, nervous smile.

I shook my head and reached between Chase and Lucy to grab a piece of cold pizza from the table. Apparently I was just going to be kept out of the loop on everything. Needing some space, I took a bite of my pizza, then walked out of the room toward the side door that led to Allison's backyard. Thoughts about Allison and Max could wait. Thoughts about Chase could wait. What was important was finding Claire's killer.

I let myself outside and instantly felt better as I was hit by the damp smell of trees. My dad's words echoed in my mind as my feet crunched over patches of snow. *Think about what makes you happy.* The problem was, I didn't know what made me happy anymore. Bringing a murderer to justice probably wasn't it, but it was worth a shot.

Devin and Lela both arrived around 10pm, and I went outside to meet them. As I watched Devin's cab drive away, I was grateful that Lela now owned her own car, as we wouldn't all fit in Allison's.

I crossed my arms as Devin and Lela both approached. I was the only one that had come outside to meet them, as everyone else was busy watching *The Shining*. Lucy had thought it would put me in a better mood. It hadn't. Before I found out I was a demon, I really enjoyed watching old horror movies. Now too many of them were a little too close to reality. It took some of the enjoyment out of it.

I moved aside for Lela to enter the house, gliding like a tall, exotic shadow. I offered her a smile and a nod as she passed me. Lela and I had never become close, but I'd actually grown to like her. She was a calming presence to be around, and she was afraid of me, so she never argued. It sounds kind of mean to enjoy someone being afraid of you, but our friendly relationship was easy, and with the current state of my life, easy was refreshing.

I moved to block Devin's way before he could walk inside. I was surprised to see him in the casual attire of a maroon button-up shirt and jeans. I'd only ever seen him in suits.

"What's with the suitcase?" I asked in greeting.

He put said suitcase down beside his feet and ran a

hand through blond hair that was almost white, just like mine and my dad's. Fortunately for Devin though, he actually had a bit of a tan, so he didn't look like a mono-chromatic ghost.

"Well I don't think we'll be solving this murder before bedtime, Xoe," he said snarkily.

"Well you should probably take your suitcase to a hotel then, Devin," I replied, mimicking his tone.

"First you make me take a cab all of the way here, and now you're not even going to give me a place to stay?" he countered.

I glared up at him. "I'm *seventeen*, so no, I don't have a spare bedroom to offer you. I don't even have a bedroom of my own, unless you count the one in the demon under-ground. You're more than welcome to stay there if you like."

Devin's face went a little green at the thought. "Fine, fine. I'll get a hotel. Now can we please go inside to discuss our plan?"

I turned around without another word and Devin followed me inside. Lela had made herself comfortable on the couch in between Chase and Lucy, while Allison and Max snuggled up on the loveseat. Without a word, Chase rose and went into the kitchen and came back with two chairs. He sat them side-by-side, forming an arch that started with the loveseat, ended with the chairs, and had the couch in the middle.

As Devin and I approached, Chase offered me his seat on the couch, then took one chair as Devin sat in the other. Allison grabbed the remote from the arm of the loveseat and muted the movie, then everyone turned to look at me expectantly.

Feeling oddly nervous to have everyone's attention on me, I began, "As most of you know, we're going to meet with the local coven tonight to discuss Claire's death. They've hired Jason to investigate, but are willing to accept our help as well."

"What does the coven have to do with any of this?" Devin interrupted.

I smiled, glad that I'd finally gotten to a piece of information before the illustrious werewolf secret society. "Claire was a witch, and her parents are part of the local coven," I explained smugly.

Devin squinted his eyes in thought. "So this murder likely has nothing to do with you," he said finally. "This is witch business, not wolf business."

I'd considered the same conclusion, but I wasn't willing to give it up that easily. "The last time witches were killed, wolves were killed too, and I came about five seconds away from getting my throat slit. It's too risky to just hope for the best."

Devin nodded, but not like he liked it. "What time do we meet with the coven?" he said tiredly.

"Midnight," I replied, losing some of my smugness at the unsettling thought of meeting with the witches. "Though it will just be you and me, everyone else will wait in the car as backup."

Devin held a hand up to his heart. "Why Xoe, I'm touched that you would think to include me."

I smiled sweetly at him. "My dad set it up. If it were up to me, you'd still be back in Utah."

He chuckled. "Now there's the Xoe I know. Where are we meeting them?"

I handed him the piece of paper my dad had given me from where it sat on the coffee table. Devin glanced at it, then shrugged. "I apologize. I didn't memorize a map of Shelby before arriving."

I smirked. "It's a residential address. That's all we know."

Devin sighed. "I assume I can at least stay here for the next hour then, or would you like me to wait outside until it's time to go?"

I leaned back against the couch, realizing that maybe I had been a little too rude upon Devin's arrival. "You can stay," I said grudgingly. "I think there's still some pizza left in the kitchen."

Suddenly no longer cranky, Devin hopped up from his seat and made his way into the adjoining kitchen, lifting his cell phone out of his pocket, presumably to report in to Abel.

Everyone left in the room looked confused over the quick exchange. I sunk down further into the couch and proceeded to pout. It was going to be a very long hour.

6

The house we pulled up to at a quarter till midnight was more of a mansion, with a high, wrought iron fence surrounding it that clearly said *keep out*. Chase and I rode in Lela's car with her and Devin, while the rest of our group followed us in Allison's car. As if by magic, the gate swung inward, and Lela pulled her car onto a huge, circular driveway, already populated by eight or nine other cars. Allison pulled in and parked right behind us.

As soon as my feet hit the gravel of the driveway I felt an almost overwhelming buzz of energy, similar to what I would normally feel in a graveyard, only amplified. I walked around to join Chase on the other side of the car. He looked down at me nervously and began humming underneath his breath. It sounded like *Que Sera, Sera,* and made me even more anxious since I knew that humming was the equivalent of a nervous tick for Chase.

"Does anyone else feel that?" I asked shakily as the rest of our group approached.

"What?" Lucy asked at the same time Max answered, "I don't feel a thing."

I looked up at Chase again, who nodded hesitantly. "If you're don't come back out within an hour, we'll come in after you."

I nodded in reply as Lela, Max, Lucy, Allison, and Chase all piled into Lela's car to wait. Devin and I approached the front door, but it opened before we could knock. We were greeted by a woman in her mid-forties, dressed in what could only be referred to as a power suit done in a monochromatic, crisp white. Her bright red hair had been blow-dried to frame her face artfully.

She offered us a warm smile with her perfectly painted, pink lips. "Welcome," she said in a voice much softer than I'd expected. "Please come inside."

At her gesture I led the way inside, with Devin following close behind me. The nameless, power suit woman turned to lead us into an open sitting room filled with a dozen more normal-looking people, including the pair I'd seen with Jason at Irvine's. I felt like my feet were stuck in mud as I walked forward, as if some unseen force was holding me back, but I managed to advance far enough to stand by Devin.

"My name is Sasha," power-suit woman announced. "The man that I spoke with said I'd be meeting with his daughter, Xoe, and her escort, Devin," she added, as if questioning who we were.

"That's us," I assured, waiting for someone to offer us a drink, or a seat, or anything you would normally do with house-guests. Instead they all just sat there and stared at us like we were something new, and maybe a little bit frightening.

The odd, electric feeling I'd felt outside increased now that I was further into the house. I felt the overwhelming compulsion to leave, and knew that it showed on my face. Something strange was going on.

Sasha's features softened as she moved to stand near a high-backed chair that hosted a small, balding man in a business suit. "I apologize for the discomfort you must be feeling," she said, surprising me. "The house is warded against evil. I wasn't sure how much it would affect you since you're half human. The magic acts as a sort of . . . repellant."

I glared at her despite how nervous I felt. Apparently to her, demons were little more than insects. "Why would a ward against evil affect me at all?"

Surprise crossed her face. She obviously hadn't realized that she'd said something insulting. "Because of your demon heritage," she blurted. "A full demon wouldn't be able to enter this house at all."

I didn't point out to her the fact that a full demon could only leave the underground in incorporeal form, and only when summoned. Any full demon besides my grandmother, that was. Portals allowed her to go wherever she pleased. I didn't doubt for a moment that if my grandmother really wanted to, she could portal into the middle of Sasha's living room no problem.

Devin gave me a worried look. I imagined he was preparing for me to lose my temper on the nice witch lady, but I felt way too weird to even think about being rude to her.

"Well," Devin said, clapping his hands together to break the uncomfortable silence. "I say we skip the formalities and get straight to business. Sasha," he said, turning toward our hostess. "We will need to question each member of your coven individually. Would you like to go first?"

Sasha's eyes widened in surprise. "Oh, I thought that we'd just tell you who we suspect, and you could question *them*."

I wanted to cut in and ask who they suspected, but Devin spoke first. "Haven't you ever heard that most people are murdered by someone close to them? The killer may not be who you suspect."

"But it was a vampire," the small bald man chimed in. "I'd say that narrows the search considerably."

I shook my head in confusion. "If you think it actually was a vampire, and not someone trying to make the murder look like it was done by a vampire, then *why* did you hire a vampire to investigate?"

Sasha's face shut down into unpleasant lines. "How do you know about that?" she snapped.

I blushed. "It's a small town. I can't help knowing the

other supernaturals who reside here." There. That was nice and diplomatic.

Sasha narrowed her eyes at me, but seemed to believe my story. It technically wasn't a lie, regardless. Still, I was surprised that the witches didn't know much about me, considering that everyone else I came across seemed to. They really were the outcasts of the supernatural world.

"We hired Jason because *he's* a suspect," Sasha replied indignantly. "Hiring him was the best route to keeping track of him, and if he's not the killer, then he's the best man to find the vampire that is."

My pulse sped a little at the accusation. I thought again of Jason's anger, but he would never hurt anyone. "Do you want our help, or not?" I snapped.

Sasha eyed me coolly. "I would not have risked inviting a demon into my house if I did not desire aid."

I walked forward confidently, ignoring the *demon* comment. "Then we do this my way. We'll question each of you individually," I said as I looked around the room. "Any volunteers to go first?"

For a moment no one raised their hands, and Sasha looked like she might step in, when a couple stood together. The man was tall, with messy brown hair and wire-rimmed glasses. He looked like a middle school teacher, and the woman looked like the principle with her neat, gray skirt suit and short, no-nonsense haircut.

"I'm Claire's mother, Cynthia," the woman announced, "and this is my husband Ben," she finished as she gestured at her partner.

I felt my confidence falter. I should have taken into account the fact that I'd have to question Claire's parents. I'm not known for my tact, and asking the poor couple about their daughter's death suddenly seemed like an extremely daunting task.

Sasha stepped forward stiffly. "You can use my office for the questioning," she said, finishing with a tight-lipped, fake smile.

Devin and I turned to follow Sasha as she led the way, with Cynthia and Ben following close behind us. I didn't like that Sasha was so against us questioning her coven. Sure, it might have been the demon thing, maybe she thought I'd eat Ben and Cynthia as soon as I had them alone, but I thought it was something else. Something stunk, and it wasn't Sasha's overpowering designer perfume.

Through a large kitchen, then halfway down a dimly-lit hall, Sasha opened a door and flipped on the light switch inside. She stood aside while Devin and I entered the room, followed by Cynthia and Ben.

When Sasha had said we could use her office, I'd expected a small room, filled with scattered papers, a computer, and other office like things. What I got was an imposingly large, dark wood desk, white carpet so plush that my feet sunk down with every step, and what looked like expensive works of art decorating the high-ceilinged walls.

Sasha waited while I awkwardly took a seat behind her desk, leaving the two upholstered chairs on the other side for Ben and Cynthia. Devin stood by my side and a little behind me like a good lackey.

Sasha opened her mouth like she would say something else, but I shooed her away with my hand. She narrowed her eyes at me, then slammed the door behind her, making the paintings rattle slightly on the walls. It was probably a bad idea to antagonize the leading witch of a coven, but she'd antagonized a demon. I wasn't the type to smite people for rudeness, in fact, I wouldn't know how to smite someone even if I tried, but she didn't know that. If she was going to be stupid, I could be stupid too.

Now that we were alone, Cynthia fiddled with her hands uncomfortably and I suddenly didn't know what to say. Devin came to the rescue, once again making me glad for his presence that night. I'd have to start being nicer to him.

"Tell us what happened the night of Claire's death," he said, getting right down to what we needed to know.

Ben patted Cynthia's hand as she started to cry. "We weren't home," he began, "and our younger daughter Rose was at a friend's house, which left Claire home alone. We don't know if she talked to anyone that night. The police questioned her friends and went through her phone, but they didn't come up with anything. Rose got home before us and found Claire. She was-" his voice cracked, and he looked to his wife for reassurance.

Instead of looking at her husband, Cynthia looked at me with pleading eyes, like she was trying to tell me something, but I had no idea what. "It was made to look like a vampire kill," Cynthia said suddenly, looking up at Devin, then back at me.

"It *was* a vampire kill," Ben corrected quickly. "All of the evidence was there."

Cynthia looked back down at her lap, defeated. I would have very much liked to talk to Cynthia alone, but wasn't sure how to go about it.

"And what evidence was that?" Devin prompted.

Ben sat up a little straighter. "The wounds," he explained, "and the missing blood."

"Missing blood?" I asked, surprised at the new information.

Ben nodded. "The cops decided that she had been killed somewhere else, and was put back in her room later. There was blood on her body, but none on her bed. With her wounds . . . " he trailed off.

"There should have been some on her bed," Devin finished for him.

"Yeah," Ben replied distantly.

I tried to catch Cynthia's eye again, but she continued to stare down at her lap. Ben eyed me suspiciously, but his attention was drawn away as Devin asked. "Do you have any enemies?"

"Of course not," Ben answered a little too quickly, looking at Devin as if clearly offended.

"What about the coven?" Devin pressed, not missing a beat.

"We are not normally involved with vampires and demons, if that's what you're asking," Ben replied indignantly. "Until our daughter's murder, I'd never even given much thought to vampires, and I definitely never thought I'd meet any *demons*."

The way Ben looked back and forth between the two of us made me realize that the witches thought Devin was a demon, which meant that my dad had probably implied it. I'd have to ask him about that later.

"You know, a lot of witches summon demons," I said suddenly.

Cynthia finally looked up from her lap to show me horror filled eyes.

"*What* exactly are you implying?" Ben asked sharply as he rose from his seat.

I raised an eyebrow at him. "I just find it strange that you could have never imagined meeting vampires and demons, but you're ready to believe that a vampire killed your daughter. Most people would assume that it was done by a human with a *Bram Stoker* obsession."

Devin put a hand on my shoulder to stop me from saying anything else. It wouldn't have stopped me, but fortunately I had said all I needed to say.

"She was *drained* of blood," he snapped, like it explained everything.

"It's not exactly difficult to remove blood from a body," I countered. "A human could have done it just as easily, or a witch." I bit my tongue as I remembered that we weren't just talking about some anonymous corpse being drained of blood, we were talking about these people's daughter.

"I was willing to give you a chance," Ben spat as he stood, "but demons truly are *evil*. You've proven that."

"Please sit down," Devin said calmly.

Ben turned his rage-filled gaze to Devin and gave him a look that would have made many a man back down, but Devin stood his ground. The stand-off ensued for several more seconds, until finally Ben sat back down, looking cowed.

"We are trying to *help* you," Devin said sympathetically. "My partner has simply spent too much time in the demon underground. She's lost her manners."

I tried to keep the confusion off my face as it clicked that Devin was trying to make me seem more scary. The scare tactics might work on Cynthia if we had her alone, but I doubted they would work on Ben.

"Vampires have to be invited in to your home!" Cynthia blurted, breaking the silence.

Ben's eyes went wide and his face turned even redder. He patted his wife's hand and said through gritted teeth, "Cynthia is having trouble with the idea that our daughter might have invited a vampire inside."

I almost shook my head, but caught myself. Vampires didn't have to be invited inside, and the statement let me know that the witches really weren't used to dealing with other supernaturals. I wasn't sure if it made me trust them more, or less.

I sighed. "Did Claire meet any new *friends* recently?"

Ben's face set into hard lines. "What is that supposed to mean?" he asked defensively.

Could I say nothing right? "Vampires like to hunt their prey," I explained, trying to not get defensive in return. "They don't just break into random houses to feed on people. Why go to the trouble? Someone wanted Claire specifically."

"Are you saying this was my daughter's fault?" Ben asked as he stood again and took a step toward the desk.

This was getting me nowhere, and I was pretty sure we had learned all that we would from our interviewees. I just stared at Ben and didn't answer.

Ben grabbed his wife's hand and pulled her up from her seat, then stormed out of the room, dragging poor Cynthia behind him.

Once the sound of their footsteps disappeared, I turned to look up at Devin. "Next time you get to be the bad cop."

Devin chuckled and looked over at the empty doorway. "They're hiding something," he said, referring to Ben and Cynthia.

I nodded. "You know, for once, I agree with you."

A moment later, Sasha strode in through the open doorway. "I think it's time that you *go*," she announced.

"Are you firing us?" I asked as I stood.

"I never even hired you to begin with!" she exclaimed as she threw her hands up in the air. "As far as I'm concerned, this has nothing to do with *you*."

I squinted at her in confusion. "Then *why* am I here? I thought you said you wanted our help."

She rolled her eyes at me. "I was told that I could meet

with *you,* or I'd have to answer to a greater demon. I chose you. Now I'm unchoosing you. I will not let demons terrorize the members of my coven."

Of course my dad had threatened her. He couldn't have just nicely offered our help. No wonder she was acting like such a, well, *witch.*

"I'll still want to question you," I said as I walked around the desk, then past her into the hallway. "I'm involved in this now, and I plan to see it through."

"Why?" she asked with a sigh.

"I'm bored," I said with a challenging look. I wasn't about to explain to her all of the reasons that I wanted to find Claire's murderer. It was simply none of her business.

"I'm free at one tomorrow," she said almost cordially, though she was probably just glad that I was finally leaving her house.

We walked back through the sitting room as the other coven members stared at us silently. Ben and Cynthia were nowhere to be seen. Sasha walked ahead to open the front door for us, then stood stiffly as Devin walked through.

She stopped me with a hand on my shoulder before I could escape. The unpleasant feeling of the house amplified with Sasha's touch, and it took everything I had to not take a step back as I turned to face her.

"You must understand, that one of our own has been killed," she explained. "Claire was like a daughter to me.

Surely the human half of you can understand why some of us are a little . . . worked up."

"Yes," I answered plainly. "The *human* side of me understands that you've all suffered a loss, but the demon side of me knows that sometimes it's humans that are capable of the greatest evil. Be careful who you trust."

Sasha narrowed her eyes at me. "You do the same." She gestured for me to leave. "Tomorrow at one. Meet me at the Blue Moon Cafe."

I stepped outside and the smothering electric feeling eased. I let out a breath as the door shut behind me. Devin had returned to Lela's car, and Lucy, Allison, and Max had gone back to Allison's car while I was speaking with Sasha, leaving me to walk across the driveway alone. I slid into the back seat of Lela's car and looked tiredly at Chase.

The clock on the dash said 12:45. Had we really only been in there for less than an hour? It had seemed like days. I knew Chase and Lela were waiting for an explanation, but I was too tired to give it to them. They would just have to wait until everyone could be filled in at once back at Allison's.

As we pulled out of the driveway, I went over a checklist in my head. First, I needed to talk to my dad to see what his take was on all that had transpired. Then I needed to talk to Jason. Part of me dreaded seeing him again and being confronted with the fact of how cold and distant he had become, but if the witches suspected him of murdering Claire, he needed to know. One of them might decide to act before I could prove him innocent.

I would try to talk to both Jason and my dad before my meeting with Sasha, another meeting I was not looking forward to. Something fishy was going on in that coven, and Sasha was at the center of it.

Chase gave me another worried glance as we drove, and I offered him a tired smile. He put a finger to each of his cheeks and lifted his mouth into a grin, making me smile for real.

"Stop being nice," I whispered. "Demons are supposed to be evil."

Chase looked a little confused, but whispered back, "Demons aren't evil, Xoe. That's just you."

I punched him in the shoulder as we both started laughing. Devin glanced over from the passenger seat at Lela. "Are they always like this?"

Lela snorted. "They're usually worse."

"This is going to be a long week," Devin replied like he was in pain.

He had no idea.

Shortly after we returned to Allison's, Lela drove Devin to the nearest hotel, and took Max home while the rest of us prepared for bed. I'd had to take a few moments to explain to everyone what had happened during the meeting with the coven, but luckily no one pressed the issue too far. Lucy and I slept in Allison's room, leaving Chase to sleep downstairs on the couch. It would have been incredibly awkward if Allison's parents decided to come home during the night, but she assured us they would be gone for another week.

As I laid my cheek against the cool pillowcase and began to drift off, I wondered if Allison ever felt abandoned by her parents being gone so much. I'd never really thought about it, and now here I was, unable to get over the fact that my mom had kicked me out of her life, when Al's parents hadn't been in her life that much to begin with. I made a mental note to be a little more considerate of Allison's situation. She never complained about it, but with my recent experiences, I knew it likely affected her more than she let on.

With that depressing thought, sleep took me.

7

I woke drenched in sweat. Oh please no. Tell me it wasn't happening again. I grabbed a pillow to press against my face as memories of the dream hit me. *Witches.* I was surrounded by witches, but I couldn't make out their faces because everything was . . . orange. I looked down to realize that I was in the middle of a campfire, which was more than a little strange. It wasn't like I was standing in it, or even in it physically, but I could see out through the flames. The witches chanted together, but I couldn't make out the words.

Suddenly I was in the dream-world, and no, not the one you go to when you sleep. The one where *dream-walkers* go to travel to different planes. I'd gone there once before to search for my grandmother. I waited at the dark, dream-world bus station for a cab, but one never came.

I groaned as I removed the pillow from my face. I was alone in Allison's room, which meant it was probably late if everyone else had already woken up. I rolled out of bed and stumbled out into the hall. I was in serious need of a shower, but coffee came first. Coffee would make everything better.

I made my way downstairs toward the scent of cooking pancakes, and yes, coffee. I reached the living room and was almost to my morning savior when I heard a knock at the front door. Allison peeked her head into the living room, and seeing me frozen mid-step, gestured for me to answer it.

Grumbling all the while, I changed course for the door, not really considering that I was still in a ratty tee shirt and flannel pajama bottoms, and probably looked like a sweaty mess. This factor was the first thing on my mind, however, when I opened the door, and there stood Jason, looking freshly washed and dressed in a hunter green flannel and jeans.

So many thoughts rushed through my head of what I should say. Sorry? Good morning? You're looking well? Nothing seemed good enough, so I just stood there feeling uncomfortable and embarrassed.

"I figured we could have that *talk* now," he said as he took in my disheveled appearance.

Now? He wanted to have our relationship talk *now*? I was *so* not ready for this. I stood there for a moment longer, then realized that I'd kept him standing on the doorstep for several minutes.

"Um, come in I guess," I said, disgusted with how meek and afraid my voice sounded.

I stood out of the way as Jason came inside. I closed the door after him, then followed him to sit on the couch. I noticed out of the corner of my eye as Lucy briefly poked her head out of the kitchen, then immediately withdrew. The illusion of privacy was nice, but Lucy would hear everything we said regardless.

I turned to Jason as he opened his mouth to speak. Panicking, I tried to think of anything I could say to delay *the talk*. "I met with the witches last night," I blurted out to delay whatever it was he planned on saying.

"*What*?" Jason asked, changing gears.

"My dad set it up," I explained quickly. "I didn't even ask him to."

Jason sighed. "What did you find out?"

I raised my eyebrows in surprise. "You're not going to lecture me about getting involved?"

Jason hunched his shoulders in defeat. "I knew you would get involved no matter what I said, especially with Devin on his way here to help. So what did you find?"

I searched his face for any sign of the frustration he'd exhibited the day before, but he looked normal. A little morose maybe, but he'd returned to the Jason I was used to.

"I'm pretty sure they're hiding something. Devin agrees," I explained, relieved that I had successfully switched the conversation to something I was more comfortable with. "Sasha seems so sure that a vampire killed Claire, and I think she expects her coven to blindly follow what she believes. Claire's dad refused to veer away from the vampire idea, even when we gave him plenty of information that should have instilled a little doubt. I think I could get more information if I could talk to Claire's mom alone. Her husband is a bully."

Jason nodded thoughtfully. "They didn't share any of their suspicions with me, so I assumed they were simply at a loss. If Sasha is so sure it's a vampire, why would she hire one to investigate?"

I bit my lip. To tell, or not to tell. "You're a suspect," I explained, "so Sasha wants to keep you where she can find you. If you're not the murderer, then you can at least help her find who is. Who better to track down a vampire than one of his or her own kind?"

Jason shook his head ruefully. "It's all coming together now. I should have seen this coming."

"She also wasn't terribly keen on me getting involved, and even had her house warded against demons. It was . . . uncomfortable."

"Well I wasn't terribly keen on getting you involved either," he said, almost smiling, "but here we are."

"Yeah," I cringed as I turned my gaze down to my lap. "Here we are."

"So we might as well work together," he added.

I looked up in surprise. "Really?"

Jason shrugged. "It would be silly not to. Our personal problems can wait."

I knew I shouldn't push it, but I'm just a button pusher. It's what I do. "I thought you said you needed space . . . " I trailed off.

Jason smiled. "I guess you do actually listen to what I say, sometimes."

I smiled too. Not wanting to lose this new found almost camaraderie, I switched the conversation back to work. "I'm meeting Sasha for coffee today at one," I explained. "It might be a good time to snoop around her house. I've got a bad feeling about that place."

He laughed. "At least you've been allowed inside. The coven seems to hold to the idea that if they don't invite me in, I won't be able to enter the house on my own. Tell me you will at least take backup to this coffee date?"

I nodded. "If you count Devin as backup, then yes."

"Good. I would go with you myself, but as long as I'm a *suspect*, Sasha probably shouldn't know that we're working together. I also agree that one of us should try to speak to Cynthia alone. Perhaps if I ask to meet with Ben, I could keep him away long enough for you to get to her."

"Perfect," I agreed.

With that, it seemed we didn't have anything else to say, and just sat awkwardly for a few moments of silence. Not wanting to talk about our relationship, but also not wanting Jason to leave just yet, I remembered my primary objective. "Coffee?" I offered.

Jason cringed. "I would, but I'm not sure how I would feel about being around you and Chase in the same room. I know it's silly."

My heart skipped a beat. "It's not silly. I understand," I mumbled, feeling ashamed.

"But we'll meet up after you're done with Sasha?" he offered hopefully.

I let out a relieved breath. "It's a . . . plan." I replied, hoping he hadn't heard my hesitation where I almost said *date*.

He smiled warmly, making me feel like the cold and distant Jason had simply been a bad dream.

"Oh wait!" I exclaimed as he began to rise from the couch. "I forgot to tell you that I had a *dream* last night."

Jason knew all about my mild gift for foretelling. He resumed his seat with a concerned look on his face.

"In my dream I was with the witches, but I couldn't see their faces. It was like I was looking out from the center of a campfire. They were all chanting, but I couldn't understand what they were saying. Then the dream switched so that I was stranded alone in the dream-world."

Jason's expression turned thoughtful once again. "Are you sure you didn't physically go to the dream-world?" he asked.

"If I had, Allison's house probably wouldn't be looking so nice," I reminded him. The only time I'd gone to the dream-world, I'd accidentally made a portal so that I went there physically. The plan had been for me to go in more of an astral projection sense.

He nodded apologetically. "I forgot about that. So I assume you haven't figured out why your portals leave destruction in your wake."

I shook my head. "I haven't even tried making one since I destroyed my mom's house."

Jason patted my hand in sympathy, and I felt a slight rush at the unexpected touch. "Do you have any idea what the dream meant?"

I shook my head. "I'm not sure, but it makes me trust the witches even less. Maybe I'm just being biased due to my past experiences, but I'm pretty sure they're up to something."

I could almost see the gears turning in Jason's head as he processed the information. After a moment he nodded to himself. "I'll see what I can find at Sasha's house while you're with her. Call me as soon as the two of you part ways."

He rose and walked toward the door, but before leaving he turned to face me. "Be careful, Xoe. Don't go anywhere alone, please."

I held up one hand in the salute for "scout's honor", and then Jason was gone. I took a deep breath, then rose from the couch to face my friends who had most likely been eavesdropping throughout mine and Jason's entire conversation.

Lucy handed me a cup of coffee as I entered the kitchen, and Allison wrapped an arm around my waist in a comforting gesture. Chase sat at the kitchen table over an untouched plate of pancakes, sipping his coffee and not meeting my eyes.

Lucy glanced back at Chase, then gestured that we should go upstairs. Lucy and Allison turned to lead the way while I watched Chase as we left, feeling torn. I for some reason felt like I needed to reassure him, but reassure him of what? Jason's visit hadn't really changed anything, and I still felt just as confused as ever.

Chase looked up just before I lost sight of him, and he looked absolutely miserable. Allison grabbed my hand to pull me forward more quickly, and then Chase was out of my sight completely.

I followed my friends upstairs to Allison's room, feeling like my steps were heavier than they should have been. As soon as we were all inside, Allison gently shut the door behind us. I felt like it was rude to just leave Chase in the kitchen like that, but looking at the concerned faces of my girlfriends, I had to admit that I *really* did need to talk.

"So you're working *together* now?" Lucy asked as we all sat on Allison's bed with me sandwiched in the middle.

I shrugged. "I guess? He didn't even seem mad anymore."

Allison snorted. "Maybe he realized that he was being an idiot, and decided he didn't want to lose you permanently."

I stared down at my lap, not sure what to say.

Lucy put a hand on my shoulder. "Unless he's already lost you?" she asked like it was a question.

I shook my head. "I don't know. It just feel . . . weird. Chase has become one of my best friends, and he's okay with how I handle things."

Allison raised an eyebrow. "Who said anything about Chase?"

I snorted. "Oh please, you were both already thinking it."

Lucy scrunched her face up in thought. "Do you think Chase would still have that attitude if you got together?"

I shrugged. "I can't even think about it right now. Jason was protective from the start. We both went into the relationship knowing who the other was. I don't understand why it suddenly became a problem."

Allison looked at me like I was being silly. "Are you blind? It was a problem from the start. He's always tried to talk you out of danger. If it were up to Jason, you'd run and hide at the first hint of things going wrong."

I hunched my shoulders, feeling miserable. Had that really been the case? "What ever happened to good ol' compromise?" I asked.

Lucy snorted. "You happened, Xoe. You wouldn't know a compromise if it bit you on the butt."

I glared at Lucy, but knew she was right. Compromise wasn't my strong suit, and it apparently wasn't Jason's. Really, most of our problems probably came not from our differences, but from us being too much alike.

Allison sighed at my expression. "I have to ask, Xoe. Are your feelings for Chase solely based on things being easy with him, about him being willing to compromise with you, or do you actually care about him?"

I felt the first tears slide down my face. I didn't have time for this. Devin would be here soon, and I needed to shower and get ready to meet with Sasha. I had a murder to solve, for crying out loud. I shouldn't be sitting around crying about boys.

I stood abruptly and started walking toward the door, ready to dismiss the entire conversation.

"Just answer the question," Allison called out.

I took a deep breath and turned partially to face her with my hand on the doorknob. "I think I love him," I said finally.

"And do you love Jason?" she pressed.

I looked down at the ground, then up again to meet her earnest brown eyes. "Yes."

Allison flopped back on the bed with a sigh. "Well, shit."

"My sentiments exactly," I mumbled as I opened the door and escaped toward the bathroom. My suitcase was already in the upstairs hall since I'd needed it to get ready for bed, so I grabbed it and hustled the rest of the way to the bathroom before anyone could stop me.

Unfortunately I ran into Chase right as he was coming out of the bathroom in nothing but a towel. We stood staring at each other blankly for a moment.

"I, um, forgot to grab my suitcase," he mumbled.

I looked down awkwardly as he moved out of the way so I could enter the bathroom. I almost made it too, but the sound of Chase clearing his throat stopped me. I turned to face him again.

"If you want me to leave . . . " he began.

My eyes widened in surprise. "Why on earth would I want you to leave?"

He blushed and looked down. "I just thought," he shook his head. "I really don't know what I thought."

Confused by his meaning, but not really wanting to push him on it, I raised my eyebrow playfully. "You'll still be here when I get out of the shower, right?"

"Well *somebody* has to keep you from getting kidnapped by witches again, so I guess I'm kind of stuck," he joked.

I snorted. "I got kidnapped by witches *one* time. What are the chances of it happening again?"

"You don't exactly have the best luck with these things," he countered.

I laughed, but it sounded weak even to me. Chase left me to find his suitcase, and I was finally able to be alone behind a locked bathroom door. I sighed as I pressed my back against the wall. I had no idea what I was going to do, and I wasn't referring to Claire's murder. For once my biggest problem was one that normal teenagers might face, yet somehow it was more terrifying than all of my demon problems combined.

Solve a murder? Sure. Lead a werewolf pack? No sweat. Follow my heart, and do what was right for *me*? Not so much.

8

By the time I showered and dressed in jeans and a lightweight, crimson blouse, Devin had arrived to go over our game plan. I would have much preferred a tee shirt, but as my dad had packed my clothes I didn't have much choice. At least I wouldn't feel like a total ragamuffin when I faced Sasha again. The thought of her perfectly manicured appearance almost made me wish I had something more dressy than jeans . . . almost.

Chase, Devin, and I sat around the kitchen table while Allison and Lucy did homework in Allison's bedroom. At first I'd felt a little smug that I didn't have to do homework too, but my smugness was soon erased by the thought that I wouldn't be getting a high school diploma either. Suddenly homework didn't seem so bad.

Devin snapped his fingers in front of my face to bring me back to reality. "Did you hear anything I just said?"

I glared at him, even though I had not, in fact, heard anything he'd just said. I was saved by the bell, as it were, as my phone started buzzing in my pocket. I retrieved it as I stood, turning my back to Devin and Chase.

Seeing my dad's name on the caller id, I answered the phone without a second thought. "Hey dad, what's up?"

"It's me, Pop Tart," Dorrie's voice whispered. "You need to get down here. I'm scared."

"Dorrie?" I asked, confused. "Why do you have my dad's phone?"

"Please come," she whispered. There was a loud crash in the background, then the line went dead.

I turned to look at Chase with my mouth agape, feeling sick with the thought that something had happened to my dad, and might at that very moment be happening to Dorrie.

"We have to go," I said numbly.

"Who is Dorrie?" Devin demanded.

Ignoring Devin, Chase rose and gripped both of my arms in his. "What happened?" he asked calmly. "Where's your dad?"

I shook my head as the numbness wore off, only to be replaced by the dire need to act. "I don't know," I tried to say calmly, but it came out more like a sob. "Dorrie was whispering like someone might hear her, and she said she was scared. I think my dad is in trouble. We have to get underground."

"But your portals . . . " Chase began.

"*Who* is Dorrie?" Devin asked again.

"It doesn't matter!" I snapped, answering both of them at once. I looked up at Chase. "We'll just have to go as far into the woods as possible and hope for the best."

"What about Sasha?" Devin snapped back, either not understanding the gravity of the situation, or else not caring.

I took a deep breath to keep from losing my temper. "*You* meet with her. I have to go."

I grabbed Chase's hand and ran out of the kitchen, leaving Devin cursing behind us. Lucy and Allison were coming down the stairs to see what the commotion was, but there was no time for an explanation. I reached the front door, flung it open, and hit the ground running. Chase followed as I circled to Allison's backyard and made my way toward an open expanse of woods, nearly slipping on patches of ice as I went. I ran until my lungs couldn't take anymore of the icy air tearing through them, then came to a skidding halt.

Chase reached my side, and turned wide eyes to me as he panted. "Are you sure we're far enough? We don't want to hit Allison's house."

"It will have to do," I panted back, looking over my shoulder to see how much space we actually had. The damage done by my portals was fairly localized, at least it had been so far. If the radius remained the same, I shouldn't hit any houses.

I gripped both of Chase's hands in mine, envisioned my dad's house, and braced myself for the almost-violent feeling of traveling by portal. Just as the world began to shift, Lucy came out of nowhere and grabbed onto our joined hands. I had a moment to look at her in astonishment, then we were airborne.

I felt incredibly dizzy, then we were standing in the middle of my dad's kitchen. Lucy stumbled away from us to throw up in the kitchen sink.

I glanced around the room cautiously. I would have liked to yell at Lucy for being so reckless, but it would have to wait. Everything seemed still and normal.

With a nervous look at Chase, we both crept forward. Everything seemed normal in the hallway as well. We walked along in silence, checking each room for my dad, but they were all empty, and there was nothing out of place that I could see. After a few minutes Lucy joined us, looking a little green, but otherwise unharmed.

The last place we checked was the bathroom, and that was where we found Dorrie. At first I'd thought that the room had been covered in glitter and concrete dust, then my mind put together the pieces. First I saw one glittering hand on the bathroom rug near my feet, then the other pieces began to take shape. I gagged, and almost lost my breakfast on the remains. She'd been shattered. Dorrie had told me once that she was hollow, and didn't have any insides, but I hadn't realized just how true that had been. The pieces of her body looked like pieces of a ceramic mannequin.

"What is all of this?" Lucy asked, confused.

She had never met Dorrie. Suddenly the magnitude of the situation hit me, and I spun around. My intent was to run to the kitchen, but I ended up collapsing to vomit in the hallway. The next thing I knew, Chase was there rubbing my back, then helping me to stand once I'd finished.

I let him pull me in against his chest as I began to sob. A slight trembling took over my body, and I felt my legs give out. Chase gripped me tighter and kept me standing, then I felt Lucy's arms grab me from behind as Chase handed me off. It was an awkward position, as Lucy is several inches shorter than me, but she managed.

I watched numbly, tears streaming down my face, as Chase bravely went back into the bathroom. It wasn't right. I'd seen death before. Heck, I'd *caused* death before, but it had never been someone that I cared about. I'd only known Dorrie for less than a month, but her death hit me like a semi truck.

Shaking my head over and over, I pushed away from Lucy to stand on my own. If Chase could bear to look at the scene, then so could I. I owed Dorrie that, at least.

I stumbled back into the bathroom, gagging again as the scene came into view. The majority of Dorrie's parts had ended up in the bathtub. She must have been hiding behind the shower curtain when they found her. But who were *they*? As I watched, Chase reached down into the basin and lifted my dad's glitter and dust covered cell phone into his hand.

"Why would anyone want to hurt her?" I asked weakly.

Chase shook his head as he began pushing buttons on

my dad's phone. "I don't know, but your dad was making a lot of phone calls over the past hour. Whatever happened went down right before Dorrie called you."

"You're saying *this* was a person?" Lucy asked, gesturing at the dust as she came to stand beside me.

"More than a person," I replied. "She was my friend."

A look of grim determination came across Chase's face as his eyes met mine. "We'll find who did this, Xoe, but first we need to find your dad."

"Where do we start?" I asked weakly.

Chase put my dad's phone in his pocket, then moved to guide Lucy and I out of the bathroom. "I recognize the last number your dad called," he explained as we went. "We'll start there."

"We have to take Lucy back first," I argued as we followed Chase down the hall.

"I'm not going back," Lucy argued. "I can help."

"There's no time regardless," Chase replied without looking back at us.

I lunged forward and grabbed Chase's arm to make him face me. "What aren't you telling me?"

Chase's expression was calculating. "The last number your father called was *the Wizard*."

I shook my head. "Is that some sort of *Lord of the Rings* reference?"

"*Wizard of Oz*," Chase corrected.

He started walking again, and soon we'd gone through the front door and out onto the street.

"*Who* is the Wizard?" I panted as I tried to keep up.

Lucy followed close behind me, looking around nervously. We weren't supposed to bring non-demons underground, and it was seriously a bad idea to let Lucy follow us out in the open, but we couldn't very well leave her at my dad's house. Not after what happened to Dorrie.

"He's a record keeper," Chase explained. "Or at least, he's supposed to be. Really he deals in black-market information."

"So he might know where my dad is?" I asked hopefully as we hurried along.

We were taking mainly back streets, avoiding the more populated areas of the demon city. Lucy sniffed the air frantically, glancing over her shoulder at every sound.

Chase nodded, but didn't look over at me. "He was the last person your father called, so at the very least we can find what information he was looking for. The Wizard's services come with a high price, so whatever it was, it was important."

I stepped to the side as a normal-looking demon child went running past us, oblivious to our dire situation.

"If his services are so pricey," I panted, "then how will we get him to tell us anything?"

Chase shook his head. "He'll talk. He'll make it a miserable experience, but he'll talk."

I wanted to stop Chase so that he would actually look at me, but I knew we couldn't spare the time. "How do you know he'll talk?" I asked instead.

Chase didn't answer, but kept walking forward, clearly a man on a mission.

"Chase!" I rasped.

"He's my brother," he snapped.

I was so shocked that I stopped walking, causing Lucy to run into my back as she was too preoccupied looking at our surroundings. When Chase didn't stop, I had to jog to catch back up.

"Say that again?" I said as I reached him.

"He's my brother," he repeated, but not like he liked it.

"How did I not know you had a brother?" I questioned. As far as I knew, Chase had mostly grown up on his own.

"You never asked," he said as he turned down a dark alleyway.

"That's not the type of thing I should have to ask to know," I whispered, feeling the need to be quiet in the unnervingly quiet alley.

Chase stopped in front of a dilapidated door in the brick of a tall building. Before I could press him further, the door opened inward without us even having to knock. Chase took a deep breath, then walked inside. With a nervous glance back at Lucy, I did the same.

"First the father, now the daughter," a voice called out from the darkness within the building. The air of the place was ice-cold, and smelled like the inside of a cave.

"We could do without the spooky atmosphere, Sam," Chase said tiredly.

A light switched on, revealing someone who looked

eerily like Chase, except that the color of his eyes was almost white, making the pupil look like it was stranded in the middle of each of his eyeballs.

"Oh you're no fun," he chided.

He stepped closer to reveal that his irises were in fact white, and his face was slightly more masculine than Chase's with a wider jaw and larger brow.

"Why did Alexondre call you?" Chase asked impatiently.

"You know my information comes with a price, brother," Sam countered as he circled us like a shark.

"You owe me," Chase replied through gritted teeth.

Lucy let out a small yip as Sam poked a finger into her side like he was testing whether or not she was real.

"It's not very smart of you to bring a werewolf down here," Sam commented casually, making Lucy gasp.

Chase sighed. "Just tell us what we want to know, and we'll all be out of your sight in no time."

Sam tsked at him. "I've been waiting all of this time to meet the illustrious Alexondra. I've heard so many interesting things. I don't want you out of my sight in no time."

"We can get together for tea later," I cut in sarcastically. "Right now, I need to find my dad."

Sam stopped his circling to stand in front of me. He was a few inches shorter than Chase, which put him at about 5'10". "I can help you with that, but nothing is free."

"What do you want?" I snapped.

"Well I see the rumors of your ill temper are true," he commented. "I want you to owe me a favor."

"No," Chase said sternly at the same time I said, "Fine."

Sam looked between the two of us irritably. "Which is it, no or fine?"

"*I'll* owe you the favor," Chase replied before I could answer.

"Nope," Sam said cheerfully. "I want my favor from Alexondra. She holds a little more sway down here than you do. Plus, brother, you've proven time and again that you are not terrible reliable when it comes to favors."

I looked up at Chase, whose face had set into angry lines. "You wanted me to extort other demons for money," he countered coldly.

Sam smirked and turned to me. "What about you Alexondra, are you squeamish about extortion?"

I smiled sweetly at him. "No extortion, no violence. You give us information now, and I'll give you information in the future."

"He already has access to everyone's information," Chase explained, but Sam held up a hand to stop him.

"No, no," Sam replied with an odd smile. "I like these terms. If I help you now, I can come to you at any point in the future, be it in a week, or in a year, and you will have to answer a question truthfully in any setting I deem fit. Deal?"

"Deal," I said.

I didn't like the way he had worded the terms so specifically, but I was more than ready to get out of the dank smelling building to find my dad. With how things had been going, I probably wouldn't live long enough for him to collect on his side of the deal regardless.

Chase bit his lip in frustration, but didn't argue.

Sam took a step back from us and closed his eerie eyes. Suddenly the energy in the room picked up, and barely perceptible, shadowy forms began to creep forward from the corners of the room.

Lucy huddled a little closer to me as I looked up at Chase. "What is he doing?" I asked nervously.

Chase looked angry, but not at all scared. "You remember how I told you that my mother was a Naga and my father was a Necro-demon?"

I nodded nervously as I turned my attention back to Sam's perfectly still form.

"I take after our mother, and Sam takes after our father," Chase explained. "The dead give him information, among other things."

I shook my head in disbelief. Whenever I began to think that I understood what demons were and what they could do, they'd go and throw me a curve ball. The shadows swirled around Sam, leaning what seemed to be their faces toward his head.

Suddenly Sam's eyes shot open, and the shadowy shapes disappeared. "I'm not going to tell you what information your father was looking for," he announced dramatically, "but I can tell you where he is now."

"So cut the show-boating and tell me," I demanded.

Sam rolled his eyes at me. "I can see why you and my

brother spend so much time together, you're both a couple of party poopers. Your father is above-ground."

I sighed. "We went through all of this to find that out?"

Sam snickered as he lifted a hand up to his mouth coyly. "He's above-ground because he was summoned."

My breath caught in my throat. Who would want to summon my dad, and what did it have to do with what happened to Dorrie?

"How do we find him?" Chase asked while I was too busy being confused.

"Another question equals another favor," Sam said playfully.

"If something happens to Alexondre because you wasted too much of our time . . . " Chase began menacingly.

Sam rolled his eyes again. "Fine, fine. He was summoned by a witch in your pathetic little town, and that's all I know. There was a protection circle involved, so he went off the radar as soon as he was summoned."

I shook my head as I thought things over, then turned to Chase. "They can't hurt him, right? When a demon is summoned, it's only in incorporeal form."

Chase still looked worried. "That's true, but they may have summoned him to keep him busy. The only reason for hurting Dorrie was to keep her from telling you what's going on."

"But why?" I pressed, still not understanding.

"Our dear, departed Bartimus wasn't the only one

who knew about your portals," Sam chimed in. "Perhaps someone still wants to use you."

"Now you decide to be helpful?" Chase snapped.

Sam shrugged. "I'll never get my favor if something happens to her."

"We need to talk to Cynthia," I stated. When Chase and Lucy both looked at me in confusion, I clarified, "Claire's mom. If it's Sasha's coven that summoned my dad, Cynthia will be our way in."

"How do you know?" Lucy asked.

I shook my head, I was mainly going on instinct, but her pleading expression from the night before kept flashing through my mind. "She had something to tell me about Claire's death, but her husband stopped her. Something fishy is going on, and Cynthia is the weakest link."

"But what does that have to do with your dad?" Lucy asked.

Sam was looking back and forth between the three of us, seemingly delighted by our conversation.

I smiled bitterly. "They're not telling us everything about Claire's death, and now they've summoned my dad. The two things are connected in some way."

"I just had a terrible thought," Chase said suddenly. "*If* your dad's summoning is a ploy to leave you unprotected, your pack and Devin could be in danger too."

I inhaled sharply at the thought. "We sent Devin to meet with Sasha alone."

Sam stepped forward. "If you destroy my home with

one of your portals right now, I'm going to be seriously ticked off."

"Do you have any better suggestions?" I asked impatiently.

"Learn to be a proper demon?" he suggested.

I glared at him in response.

He shrugged. "Worth a shot. You could also just go and destroy one of the many *abandoned* buildings on this lot."

I gestured toward the door we'd come in through. "Lead the way."

Sam sighed. "Must I do everything?"

"Yes," Chase answered.

With another sigh, Sam led us back into the alleyway, then took his sweet time walking past several more shady looking doors until finally stopping by a doorway that only had half a door left to it.

He nodded at the door as if satisfied. "This should do." He turned to face me, "I'll be in touch," he stated, then turned and walked back toward his own dilapidated door.

"Sam!" I called out before he could disappear into his little cave.

He turned back and looked at me with an odd smile.

He'd already stated that he wasn't going to tell me everything I needed to know, but I couldn't let him go without asking, "What information was my father looking for?"

He stood motionless for a moment, then his creepy

little smile crept back onto his face. "He wanted information on *you*," he called back.

Sam finished the walk to his door and disappeared inside while I stood staring after him with my jaw agape like an idiot. He wanted information on . . . me? I was his daughter, what information was left to know?

I shook my head in confusion as Chase set to prying the remaining half of the door away. Lucy stood close to my side, looking up at me with a worried expression. Before she could inevitably ask what Sam had meant, the remainder of the door came loose and we walked inside. The interior had obviously hosted many squatters, as was evident by the heaps of fabric, newspaper, and empty food cans.

"Do you smell anyone else here?" I asked Lucy, worried that I would end up killing some unsuspecting hobo demon.

Lucy shook her head. "I smell *a lot* of things, but I don't think any of them are living."

I took a deep breath and reached out one hand to Chase and one to Lucy, preparing for takeoff. As soon as their fingers were safely intertwined with mine, I thought of Allison's living room, glad that I would only destroy the place I was leaving, and not the place I was going to.

Moments later we stood before a stunned Allison and Max as Lucy stumbled off to the bathroom.

"What the heck!" Allison shouted as soon as she regained her composure.

"Where's Devin?" I asked, ignoring the infuriated look on Allison's face. "Did he already meet with Sasha?"

"Oh he won't be meeting with her anytime soon," she said with dramatic flair.

It was only then that I realized how freaked out Max and Allison looked, way more freaked out than our sudden appearance merited.

Devin walked in from the kitchen with his cell phone in hand. I breathed a sigh of relief to see him. I would have never forgiven myself if he walked into a trap because of me.

"Sasha is dead," he stated. "I went to the coffee shop, but when she didn't show, I came back here, only to find your vampire here as well. Apparently you had schemed for him to investigate her house. Well, he found more than he bargained for, in the form of Sasha's body, mutilated just like the girl's."

I shook my head in disbelief. I had been so sure that Sasha was behind whatever was going on. "Where's Jason?" I asked numbly.

"He went to search for the dead girl's father," Devin replied like it didn't really matter.

I clenched my fists in frustration. "He was *supposed* to wait so I could talk to Cynthia."

"Well he had to notify *someone* that the head of their coven is dead, and I think we can all agree now that this is most definitely witch business and not *our* business."

In that moment, it was very difficult for me to not light

Devin on fire. Funny, since just a moment before I was overwhelmed with joy to see him alive.

"Someone summoned my dad, and . . . *killed* my friend," I explained, choking up as my thoughts returned to Dorrie.

Devin sighed. "It just couldn't be easy, could it? Not with you involved." He turned to go back into the kitchen. "I have some calls to make, don't go running out of here all half-cocked again."

I was tempted to do just that, but instead followed Lucy and Chase's lead as we went to sit in the living area with Allison and Max. I pulled out my cell phone and looked through my recent calls for Jason's number. It wasn't hard to find, since I'd called it a hundred times while he was missing. Pushing back the uncomfortable feelings of that thought, I put the phone to my ear and let it ring.

I let out a sigh of relief when I heard his voice on the other end of the line. He couldn't find Claire's parents, or any of the other witches for that matter. I told him everything that had happened on my end, and he hung up with a promise that he was on his way.

I leaned against Lucy and put my head on her shoulder as my adrenaline subsided. We all sat in silence and waited, because there was nothing else we could do.

9

My phone buzzed while we waited, and I was so shocked by the caller ID that I almost forgot to answer it. Putting down the cold piece of pizza I was eating, I fumbled into action as I pushed the green button and held the phone up to my ear. "Mom?" I questioned.

"Hey ... honey," she said hesitantly. "A woman named Cynthia is here to see you. She says you and her ... daughter were classmates. She seems upset."

The way that she hesitated before saying daughter let me know that my mom knew about the murder. Of course, it was a small town. *Everyone* knew about the murder. The warring emotions that suddenly overtook me were a little too much. My mom had finally made contact ... but only because Cynthia was there. At the same time, holy crap, we'd found Cynthia.

"Is it okay if I come there?" I asked awkwardly.

"S-sure," she stammered. "We'll see you soon."

"Okay," I answered as I tried not to cry. "See you soon."

I ended the call and stared blankly ahead. After weeks of not speaking, I was finally going to see my mom.

"Xoe?" Lucy questioned. "*Xoe?*" she said again when I didn't answer. "If Cynthia is there, we should go," she said finally.

I startled back into reality. Of course Lucy had heard everything my mom said, which meant she had heard everything my mom *didn't* say. I felt almost embarrassed for some reason, like there should have been some great, heartfelt reunion for my friends to listen in on.

I shook my head. "You guys should call Lela and wait here together. If this is about me, then I'm not going to drag you all into it."

"But-" Lucy began.

"*No,*" I snapped. "If anything happens, I'll make a portal and escape with my mom, but I can only bring along so many people. It's safer for me to go alone."

Chase put a hand on mine. "You're not going alone," he stated.

"This is *my* problem," I argued. "I get to choose how I deal with it."

"Your father is my friend," he stated defensively, "and so was Dorrie. I'm coming with you. Deal with it."

"Fine," I snapped as I stood.

Devin walked back into the living room, looking frustrated. "You are *not* leaving again."

I turned to fully face him. My dad was missing, Dorrie was dead, and now my mom could very well be in danger. I'd had enough. I stared Devin down. "You can try stopping me, but I don't advise it," I said calmly.

Devin huffed in annoyance, and turned to look at Lucy, Allison, and Max. "I assume you will all back up the story that I did everything in my power to stop her?"

"Sir, yes sir," Max said weakly, as Allison and Lucy nodded.

Now that things were settled, I stormed up to the front door. Tears stung at my eyes, but I wouldn't let them win. I flung open the door only to find Jason waiting on the other side.

"Cynthia is with my mother," I stated. "Don't you *dare* try and stop me."

Jason took one look at my tear-stained face and nodded. "Let's go."

I didn't argue about him coming. I knew it was in my power to make the others stay, but with Chase and Jason, it would have just been a waste of precious time.

I left the doorway and was glad to see Jason's car parked out front. With the emotional stress on my brain, I hadn't even thought about *how* Chase and I would get to my mom's. We could have walked, but it would have taken too much time.

We piled into the car without another word. I took the passenger seat while Jason drove, and Chase sat in the back. In any other situation, being alone with the two boys would have made me feel incredibly awkward, but at that moment, all I could think about were my parents.

"Where is your father?" Jason asked as we drove.

I glanced at his stony expression, but he kept his eyes on the road. "How much did Devin tell you?"

"He said you got a call from someone, and rushed off to the underground."

Devin *would* make it sound that simple. "He's missing. Someone summoned him, and . . . hurt Dorrie."

Jason shook his head. "Just once I had hoped that things wouldn't be about you, but you really *are* always in danger."

"She's one of only two demons in existence that can make portals," Chase cut in. "Rare things are always in danger."

Anger crept across Jason's face. "If she wouldn't have gotten involved with the wolves, no one would even know about her."

I looked at him in surprise, because what he said was just plain untrue. "Bart sent Nick and the witches after me based on the fact that my grandmother could make portals, and he hoped I could too. There was nothing I could have done to stop that."

Jason clenched his jaw, but didn't respond.

"I think you just *want* this all to be my fault, because it makes it easier for you to deal with," I accused.

"What is that supposed to mean?" Jason asked. "I don't *want* to be mad at you."

I snorted. "You may not want to be mad at me, but it's

easier than being mad at fate or whatever else you want to call it. You're mad because I am what I am, and it makes life difficult. This whole time I've been feeling bad about how my life affects *you* and everyone else, but try living it."

Jason smacked his palm against the steering wheel in frustration. "It doesn't *have* to be this way."

"But it does!" I shouted. "There is *nothing* wrong with who I am, and if you can't deal with it, that's *your* problem."

Jason turned sharply into my mom's driveway and brought the car to a skidding halt. I got out and slammed the door shut, followed by Chase, who didn't slam his door. I half-expected Jason to drive away, but he got out and shut his door too.

He took a deep breath and let it out before looking over at me. "You're right."

"I-I'm what?" I asked, confused.

"You're right. Let's go talk to Cynthia."

He began walking toward the house before I could say anything. I gave Chase a worried look, then followed.

It was strange to walk up to a house that had been my home for so many years, while feeling like I didn't belong there. My mom answered the door almost immediately, then stood aside for us to enter. It had only been a short time since I'd last seen her, but her curly, brown hair seemed longer to me, and she was wearing a casual, green dress that I had never seen. She seemed almost like a stranger, and the feeling was only increased by her closed-off stance.

As I passed her she met my eyes, looking like she wanted to say a million different things, but what came out was, "I didn't expect you to get here so quickly."

I nodded. She'd probably assumed I was in the underground when she called. "We were at Allison's," I explained.

Cynthia was sitting on the couch, looking small and scared. She looked vastly different in jeans and a pale pink flannel shirt with her hair pushed back from her face, as opposed to her polished appearance the night before.

"I'm sorry for coming here," she said quietly. "I just didn't know where else to go. I don't know who I can trust."

"Where's Ben?" I asked as I sat down beside her, trying my best to appear sympathetic.

Cynthia shook her head over and over again as she began to cry. "We were only trying to protect Rose," she sobbed.

I looked back to where Chase and Jason stood. My mom stood awkwardly behind them and a little off to the side. She glanced down at Cynthia, then met my gaze. "I'm going to make some coffee," she offered. She turned and hurried into the kitchen.

I looked back to Cynthia. "Start from the beginning please."

She looked up at me with puffy eyes. "Promise me

you'll help first. I know it was wrong, but we didn't know what would happen."

I bit my lip. I couldn't really promise to help if I didn't know what I was promising to help *with*, but I needed her to talk.

"I promise," I assured.

"Even though you're a demon?" she asked hopefully.

"I can't help if you don't tell me what's going on," I replied, getting more than a little frustrated.

"We've been summoning demons," she admitted, then waited for my reaction.

"I figured as much. Go on."

Her eyes widened in surprise at my reaction, but it seemed to give her the confidence to go on. "We weren't just *summoning* them though. Sasha found a way to actually bring a demon over entirely, not just in incorporeal form. I don't know how she did it. She wouldn't tell her secret to any of us."

My jaw dropped in surprise. "Why on earth would you want to do that? No offense, but I've met quite a few demons, and you would have to be a total idiot to want to hang out with them."

Cynthia began crying again. I waited for her to cry it out, not sure if offering comfort was the right thing to do. She might not want a *demon* to touch her. Eventually my mom walked in with several cups of coffee on a small tray. She handed each of us a mug in turn, and when she got to Cynthia she had to lift Cynthia's hand to put the mug in it. As soon as my mom's role as hostess was fulfilled, she hurried back into the kitchen. Feeling shaky, I took a steadying sip of my coffee and patted Cynthia's shoulder awkwardly.

"Sasha thought she could control them," she explained, referring to the demons. "We took so many precautions."

"That doesn't explain *why* you were summoning them," I pressed.

Cynthia shook her head, causing wisps of her short hair to fall forward onto her face. "We'd been receiving threats, and we needed a way to protect ourselves. Being able to control demons was going to be our way of being just as scary as all of the other supernaturals."

I wanted to wring her neck and demand to know if they had summoned my dad, but I resisted. Instead I asked, "Who was threatening you?"

"Werewolves," she replied simply.

I wasn't sure what answer I expected, but werewolves wasn't it. Rogue wolves were strictly policed by the coalition. Since the punishment for harming a human was a swift death, they didn't step out of line often.

"Did you report it to the coalition?" I asked, wondering if Abel knew anything about it.

Cynthia shook her head. "The other wolves would have killed us. The whole reason they were threatening us to begin with was to make us fight on their side."

I took another sip of my coffee in an attempt to keep my cool. After a moment, I asked, "What do you mean, *their side*? Who are they fighting against?"

"The coalition," Cynthia said as if it was obvious.

Suddenly everything clicked into place. Abel had pushed for me to become a pack leader because having a demon on his side made the coalition more imposing. I'd just thought Abel wanted me as a precaution, but maybe there was more to it. These rogue wolves wanted the witches to help them fight against a coalition that employed demons, and the witches wanted demons to help them fight the rogue wolves. Yet none of this explained where my dad was.

"Cynthia," I began calmly. "What happened to Claire?"

She began crying anew. I reached over and grabbed a box of tissues from the coffee table and handed them to her. She took one and dabbed daintily at her nose, then looked back up at me. "One of the demons got loose and killed her."

I shook my head. "And you all pretended it was a vampire to cover your own butts."

Cynthia began to tremble, and squeezed her eyes shut for a moment. "Sasha thought that if we hired Jason to investigate, no one would suspect that we knew what happened." She glanced apologetically over her shoulder at Jason. "I didn't want to lie. I'd already lost my little girl, but Sasha said it was the only way to protect Rose from our mistake."

I patted Cynthia's hand in an awkward attempt at comfort, though what I really wanted to do was slap her.

Even if she didn't want to, she'd lied to cover up her daughter's death. It just didn't sit right with me.

"Were you there when the demon . . . hurt her?" I asked awkwardly.

Cynthia shook her head a little too quickly. "No, Claire went to Sasha's. She went there a lot after school. When Sasha came home, she found her . . . and the demon was gone. Some of the other coven members brought Claire home. After that we warded all of our homes against evil."

The wards obviously didn't help Sasha, but I didn't say so out loud. I was too shocked that they'd actually moved Claire's body to cover up the real story of her death. In a way I understood. If they'd called the police then, Sasha would have been investigated, but it still didn't make it right.

"What do you mean, warded against *evil*?" I asked as an idea came to me. Sasha had claimed that the wards were for demons.

Cynthia scrunched her brow in confusion. "We warded against evil to keep demons out. The only reason you could cross them is because you're half human."

I shook my head. "And you really believe that full demons are pure evil?"

Cynthia squinted her puffy eyes at me and waited for me to explain what I was talking about.

"Sasha's dead, Cynthia," I said bluntly.

"B-but how?" Cynthia asked, truly shocked.

"The demon went into her house and killed her," I

explained. "Demons have a choice between good and evil, just like humans, and this demon obviously isn't purely evil."

Really, until I knew about the wards I hadn't known that pure demon didn't equal pure evil. My dad, Chase, and I all had human blood, and part of me believed that it was just our humanity that saved us from being monsters . . . but maybe I was wrong.

"Someone summoned my father and hurt my friend today," I admitted while Cynthia was still processing Sasha's death. "I need you to tell me what you know about it."

Cynthia shook her head frantically. "We haven't summoned any demons since the one escaped, I swear."

I glanced back at Chase. He gestured that we should speak outside. Seeing the exchange, Jason approached to take my place beside Cynthia. I let the gratitude show in my face as he sat down, and he offered me a small smile in return.

I followed Chase to the door, pausing by the kitchen long enough to see my mom huddled in the corner sipping her cup of coffee. I walked outside feeling even lower than I'd felt all day.

"None of this makes sense," Chase stated as soon as we were alone on the front porch. "Dorrie was hurt in the underground, so another demon has to be involved. If the witches summoned your dad, there would have been nothing for Dorrie to see, so there wouldn't have been a reason to get her out of the way. This isn't just about a werewolf turf war."

"There *has* to be another demon involved," I agreed, seeing it as the only explanation.

Chase nodded. "I hate to say this, but we should probably speak to my brother again."

I nodded in return. "We also need to find this loosed demon. If it went back and killed Sasha, it might be after the other coven members next."

I turned as my mom peeked her head out the front door. "Am I interrupting something?"

"N-no," I stammered. "What do you need?"

She left the doorway and came to stand beside me. She had put on a tan, shearling coat against the cold, and she picked at the sleeves nervously. "Are you in trouble, Xoe?"

I was suddenly at a loss for words. With how she'd been acting, I really hadn't expected her to ask what was going on. "Not directly," I admitted, "but dad is missing, and some of Cynthia's friends might be in danger." There. Nice and simple.

Her eyes widened in surprise. "And it's up to you to help them?" she asked, sounding like a little kid.

I nodded. "It's up to me to try."

She turned to Chase and gave him a scrutinizing look. "But you'll be there with her, keeping her safe?" she asked.

Chase looked a little surprised by the question. "O-of

course," he stammered. "I always do my best to keep Xoe safe."

Part of me wanted to interject that I could keep myself safe, but if my mom felt better with the idea of Chase protecting me, then I'd just have to let it go.

My mom nodded and mumbled, "Good, good."

I took that moment to finally actually look at my mom, without the distraction of Cynthia and everything else going on. She looked thinner than I'd ever seen her, and had heavy bags under her eyes. It dawned on me then that I had probably ruined my mom's life. She had done her best to create a safe home for us, and had wanted nothing more than for me to succeed and be happy. I'd destroyed that safe environment, and was pretty sure that I'd let her down on the other two counts as well. As a high-school drop out without a job, I wasn't exactly successful . . . and happy? I'd need to evaluate my life a little more before I could even begin to answer *that*.

With another nod, my mom excused herself with her arms wrapped tightly around her torso, walking as if in a daze. Chase gave me a worried look as she went back inside the house. As the door shut behind my mom, I found myself once again without words, and tears stung at the back of my eyes. As the first one fell, Chase wrapped me up in his arms. The comforting gesture made my tears fall harder, and soon my body was wracked with silent sobs. I tried to take deep breaths, but the tears just kept coming as the feelings about my mom that I'd been ignoring came to the surface.

I heard the door open behind us, then I heard footsteps on the porch as the door shut, but whoever stood there didn't speak. Fearing the worst, I pulled away from Chase to see Jason standing a few feet away. At first his face held anger, but as he took in my disheveled appearance his features softened. Likely guessing why I was crying, he didn't press the subject.

"Cynthia claims she doesn't know anything else," he explained. He took a few steps forward to stand close to us. "But I think we should follow her. She may lead us to the other witches."

"Why come to us at all if she's just going to lie?" I whispered back.

"Later," he mouthed, before turning to go back inside.

I tried to see if Chase was just as confused as I was, but he wouldn't quite meet my eyes. Instead, he led the way back inside. Cynthia had gathered herself and stood as we entered. If it weren't for the puffy eyes, you'd have never even guessed that she was a nervous wreck just a few moments before.

"You're going?" I questioned.

"I have to find Rose," she explained curtly. Her facade of steadiness almost cracked at the mention of her living daughter's name, but she managed to hold it together.

"We'll do our best to help," I assured. "Please call us if you find anything."

Cynthia's expression faltered. "You really aren't mad that we summoned demons?" she asked weakly.

I squinted at her in confusion. "I think you're a bunch of idiots, but you're already paying for your mistakes."

Cynthia nodded and started walking toward the front door, but I grabbed her arm to stop her as she walked by.

Her eyes went wide as she looked at my hand on her arm. "Please," she pleaded, "I just want to find my daughter."

I smiled, but knew it held little warmth. "I want you to find your daughter too, but I have a message for your coven, should you encounter any of them."

Cynthia stayed silent and continued to look up at me nervously.

"I think one of them summoned my dad. Normally I wouldn't be terribly worried, but if it's true that you can summon demons fully, well, that worries me. I want you to tell anyone you see that if anything happens to him, they will have to answer to me personally. I may not seem as scary as a demon that rips people's throats to shreds, but I assure you, I am quite capable of burning your lives to the ground."

Cynthia nodded a little too quickly and tried to pull away, but I held on. "You'll spread the word?" I asked.

She took in a shaky breath. "If I see any of them, they'll know what you said."

I nodded and let go of her arm. She escaped through the front door, slamming it behind her.

"Let's go," Jason said quickly as he watched Cynthia through the windowed part of the door. "We don't want to lose her."

I searched frantically for my mom, wanting to at least say goodbye, and found her huddled back in her original position in the adjoining kitchen. She regarded me with a stunned expression.

"You threatened that woman," she accused.

I stared at her, wanting to offer some sort of explanation that would make her stop looking at me like I was a monster, but what came out was, "And I meant it."

10

As we trailed Cynthia in Jason's car, doing our best to evade her sight, I called Devin to fill him in on what had happened. I told him about the demon on the loose, and about the rogue wolves hoping to overthrow the coalition.

After a few moments of stunned silence he said, "I need to call Abel. He's already on his way here, but now I'm thinking it might be a trap."

"What do you mean?" I asked before he could hang up.

"I mean that what if the witches didn't all disappear because of the demon, what if they disappeared because of the wolves? If they got wind that I was already here investigating, then kidnapping the witches would be the perfect way to lure Abel here too. They might be trying to escalate the situation."

I shook my head. It wasn't that I thought he was

wrong, but there was so much more going on that we didn't understand. "Call Abel, and have Lela come back to Allison's. You're safer together. I'll let you know if Cynthia leads us to anything. If not, Chase and I are going back underground to search for more information."

"Deal," Devin said, then the line clicked off.

I set my phone in my lap and watched as Cynthia took another turn, then pulled up into the driveway of a normal-looking house.

Jason drove past the driveway, then parked a few houses down. I looked to him for guidance as he switched off the ignition. If I had to make a choice, we would storm in after Cynthia and demand to know what was going on, but there were probably better ways to get information.

Affirming my thoughts, Jason stopped me before I could undo my seat belt. "I'll sneak around the house and see what I can hear," he explained.

I nodded, and in the blink of an eye Jason was out of the car making a beeline for the house that Cynthia had gone into. I looked over my shoulder at Chase, feeling anxious.

"I've been thinking about something," he began after he had my attention.

I nodded for him to go on.

"If these witches are powerful enough to keep your dad from returning to the underground, they were either highly misleading, or the demon is actively helping them."

I nodded again, thinking of Dorrie. "And actively hurting my friends to keep us from finding out about it."

Chase gave me a sympathetic look, then continued, "The question is, what demon would have anything to gain by releasing a lesser demon to kill witches, then making the witches summon your dad?"

"Why do you say *lesser demon*?" I asked, never having heard the term.

"If a demon like Bart had been released, the chaos would have been either much more noticeable, or we wouldn't have seen anything at all," he explained. "This demon is wasting its time picking off the witches that summoned it, one by one. It either doesn't have the power to take them all out at once, or has no other goal than petty revenge. I'm guessing it's someone not very powerful, and probably not very smart."

"So back to the demon or demons that hurt Dorrie . . . " I trailed off, wondering where Chase was going with the conversation.

Chase nodded. "The only thing that a demon would have to gain from orchestrating all of this is chaos, and all this chaos is centered around you. Releasing a violent lesser demon into your hometown would draw your attention and bring you above-ground. Then, detaining your dad and harming Dorrie would keep you from finding out what they're planning."

I shook my head, seeing another option. "I agree that I'm somehow involved, but so are the wolves. This all started because the rogue wolves wanted something to counter the demonic presence that I bring to the coalition."

"But the wolves had no way of knowing that the coven would try to summon demons themselves," Chase countered.

"Unless Cynthia lied about threat of the wolves," I countered right back. "What if the witches were working willingly with the rogue wolves, but when things got out of hand they wanted an excuse for their actions, so Cynthia lied and said the wolves threatened them?"

"That still doesn't explain what happened to Dorrie," Chase argued. "There is a demon orchestrating this, and that points to this all centering around you."

"Maybe another demon noticed what was happening and decided to take advantage, then when they realized that my father and I were already involved with the situation, they tried to cover their tracks," I offered. "Or *maybe* the witches did summon another demon in addition to the one who got loose, and maybe this demon was more than they bargained for as well. The witches could have initially been working for or against the wolves when they bit off more than they could chew. A demon might have just swooped in to take over the show."

Chase nodded in agreement as she shrugged out of his faded green jacket to reveal a loose, heather gray tee shirt. "We need to talk to Sam again, and this time we'll ask the right questions."

"Has your brother always been such a pain?" I asked,

thinking about what it might cost us to squeeze any more answers out of him.

"Yes," Chase answered simply.

"Are you ever going to tell me what happened between the two of you?" I prodded.

Chase sighed and offered me a crooked smile. "Maybe once all of this is over and we finally have a quiet moment to breathe."

"So in other words, never?" I asked bitterly.

Chase laughed just as Jason reappeared beside the car. He got in without a word and started the engine.

"What did you find out?" I asked as we began to drive away.

"She was meeting with her husband," Jason explained, "and she told the truth about not being able to find her daughter."

I felt instantly deflated. "So we still have nothing to go on?"

Jason focused on the road as we quickly escaped the neighborhood. "Not quite. She told the truth about not being able to find Rose. She doesn't know where she is, but she *does* know who took her."

"*And*?" I pressed when he didn't answer.

"She was kidnapped by the other members of her coven," Jason explained. "They're using her as collateral to keep Ben and Cynthia from ratting them out."

I looked out at the road in thought. They really were trying to protect their daughter. We were just wrong about who they were protecting her from. Too bad they hadn't done the same for Claire.

"So our next step is to find the coven," I stated, "and hopefully that will not only lead us to my dad and Rose, but to the demon that we're going to have to kill for causing us all of this trouble."

"And we're sure that it's a demon?" Jason asked.

"Yes," Chase and I said in unison.

Without asking, Jason drove back in the direction of Allison's. I didn't mind, as we needed to regroup, and if Abel would be arriving soon, he could lend his resources to our search. I wasn't particularly looking forward to seeing Abel, I was sure there would be lectures aplenty, but he was also my dad's friend, so I knew he would help me find him if he could.

Jason glanced at me like he wanted to say something, then bit his lip instead.

"What?" I prompted, as I considered too late that maybe whatever he had to say, he didn't want to say in front of Chase.

He glanced at me again, then back to the road. "I imagine that you'll be going back underground if we find no other leads on the witches?"

I shrugged. "It's the only option I see. It would probably be wise for us to go as soon as possible while the wolves look for leads, really."

"*Us*?" Jason asked casually as he picked imaginary lint off the sleeve of his flannel shirt.

"Chase and I," I clarified.

Everyone in the car went silent as I realized I had somehow put my foot in my mouth again. I mean, I knew that things were awkward, but I was just being practical.

"You know," I began, "because we're both demons, and we'd be going to the demon underground? Plus, we're going to see his brother."

Chase stayed silent while Jason nodded, but there was still a tension to his face that made me uncomfortable. "You're right," he said finally. "Your plan make sense." After a moment more he glanced back at Chase and added, "I didn't know you had a brother."

"We don't exactly get along," Chase explained.

Jason nodded again as he pulled the car into Allison's driveway. The sky was already growing dark, and I wasn't surprised that the entire day had gone by. It had felt like ten different days jumping from one emergency to the next. I didn't like the idea of re-visiting Sam during the night, his run-down abode was creepy enough when the underground was lit up with artificial daylight. I didn't want to see those eerie shapes again in the dark. Still, I couldn't just go to sleep while my dad was still missing.

We blocked in a silver car I'd never seen before that was parked behind Allison's car, and next to Lela's. It looked like we were having a party.

We exited the car and went inside to find Max, Allison, Lucy, Lela, Devin, Abel, and several people I didn't know all gathered into the living room, which had been rearranged to look more like a conference room with extra chairs all gathered together.

Abel and Devin were deep in conversation, with Lela and the strangers standing around them. They barely even acknowledged us as we entered the room. I went to stand by Allison, who stood in the corner with her arms crossed, looking irritated.

"Are you sure it's okay to have all of these people in your house?" I whispered.

She rolled her eyes at me. "It's not like *I* invited them." I was about to apologize, but suddenly she smiled. "It *would* be fun though if my parents actually came home early to find a house full of adults waiting for them."

I raised an eyebrow at her. "Fun?"

Allison smiled a little wider as she looked at her unwelcome guests. "Yes, fun," she repeated.

I shook my head as Chase approached. "Should we get going?" he asked as he reached us.

"Get going?" Allison questioned before I could answer him.

Lucy and Max approached to see what we were talking about.

"Back underground," I explained as our group came together. "We think there's another demon involved in all of this, and we want to try and get more information."

Jason joined our group last, coming to stand between me and Allison.

"And what are the rest of us supposed to do?" Max asked, sounding slightly annoyed himself, though I wasn't sure why.

"What's got your fur all ruffled?" I asked instead of answering him.

Max sighed. "We've just been stuck here all day with Devin while he makes a million phone calls, when we could actually be *helping*."

I took a deep breath to steady my own sudden annoyance, but wasn't entirely successful. "Well I'm sorry that my dad is missing and my friend was murdered, and I didn't quite have the time to consider the fact that you didn't want to sit inside all day."

Allison wrinkled her forehead at my bad attitude, but didn't say anything.

Max looked suddenly embarrassed as he said, "I'm sorry, Xoe. I only wanted to help."

Jason put his hand at the small of my back and began rubbing it in small circles. It was what he usually did when my temper reared its ugly head, but for the first time it made me feel worse. It wasn't fair for him to be cold one moment, then affectionate the next. I had enough confusion to deal with without him adding to it.

As an excuse to pull away, I turned to see if Abel and Devin had finished their conversation. They hadn't, but I was tired of waiting. I left my group and marched up to Abel, who was dressed more normally than I had ever seen him, in jeans and a hunter green sweater. His long, dark hair, pulled back into a braid, accentuated his strong, amber features.

"Alexondra, I see you've gotten us into a pickle once again," he said as he turned to face me.

Devin's shoulders relaxed as Abel's attention was taken from him, making me think they'd been discussing something that Devin was uncomfortable with.

I raised my hands in defense. "I don't think I started this one. I was just hanging out in the underground, minding my own business."

Abel gave me a scrutinizing look. "If you didn't start it, then who?"

I told him the scenarios that Chase and I had come up with in the car, and what we'd learned from following Cynthia.

He looked weary as I finished. "The rogue wolves must be our primary objective," he announced. "Without them, the witches will no longer be a problem."

"Uh," I began, surprised by his attitude. "There's also a murderous demon on the loose, and let's not forget that my dad is *missing*."

Abel looked at me like I was being silly. "I'm sure Alexondre is quite capable of taking care of himself."

I shook my head. "There is an unknown demon involved. We have no idea what he or she might be capable of."

Abel thought for a moment, then nodded. "Well then you can take care of *that* while the rest of us see to the wolves."

I opened my mouth to argue, but realized he'd suggested exactly what I'd been thinking. "Well then okay," I replied, jumbling my words.

Devin squinted at me from behind Abel's back. There

was something else going on there, but I didn't have time to worry about it. With a final nod, I returned to my friends and explained the plan to them.

"I'm coming with you," Jason said immediately.

"We're not supposed to take non-demons into the underground," I countered. "We'd be putting you in danger for no reason."

"You took Lucy," he countered.

"Lucy was a stowaway," I argued. "She jumped a ride and I didn't have time to stop her."

Lucy blushed at that, but didn't argue.

"Whoever is doing this took your father, and murdered your friend," Jason stated. "You shouldn't go back down there without backup."

I hated to say it, but he was right. I just didn't like the idea of endangering him to protect me, especially since he'd made me feel so miserable about doing it in the past.

"Fine," I said through gritted teeth. "Let's go."

As the three of us went for the front door, leaving my tired and cranky friends behind, my stomach growled. It had been several hours since I'd last eaten, but it would have to wait.

The night air that hit me as we walked through the door was much colder than usual, making me wish I'd grabbed a jacket. I run extremely warm because of my demon bloodline, but the air was chilly enough that goosebumps erupted across my bare arms as I walked slightly ahead of the two boys.

I had a feeling that if the three of us stayed together

much longer, a confrontation was bound to happen. You could cut the tension in the air with a knife.

We reached the area where Chase and I had departed from previously, and I stopped and held out a hand to each of the boys. The trees surrounding the area looked like they had been hit with giant baseball bats, and many of them had been reduced to splintered stumps. Anyone who happened upon the area would likely be monumentally confused. As for me, I just felt a little sick.

I paused for a moment as each of the boys interlaced their fingers with mine. Though their hands felt solid, the moment felt incredibly surreal with the three of us standing in the dark forest together. I shook away the odd feeling. The important thing was finding my dad. My own feelings would have to wait.

11

We landed in the middle of Sam's barren dwelling with barely a sound. If only my departures could be so in-obtrusive. I looked around the dark building, but didn't see Sam anywhere.

"Of course he chooses *now* to go somewhere," Chase commented.

"Where do you think he went?" I asked as I paced around the small space.

There was a desk in the corner that I hadn't seen before, and I went to it, hoping that maybe it held whatever information my dad had been looking for. If I could find it, we wouldn't need to wait for Sam at all.

"I wouldn't do that," Chase remarked before my hand could touch the desk.

I paused mid-motion to glance at him. "Why not?"

Chase took a few steps forward and ushered me away from the desk. "He wouldn't just leave his records unattended. My guess is that desk holds some very unpleasant surprises for any would-be information thieves."

I glared at the desk, frustrated that the information I needed was so near, but not within my reach.

"I know of a few places he might be," Chase explained, answering my earlier question, "but someone should stay here in case he comes back."

"Splitting up doesn't seem like a good idea," Jason cut in. "Especially if one person will be on their own."

"We don't have time to argue about it," I stated. "Chase and I will go, and Jason, you wait here."

Jason opened his mouth to argue, but Chase beat him too it. "Xoe, you should be the one to stay here."

I shook my head, feeling somehow betrayed. "Why?"

"We don't know what demon is behind this, and they already hurt Dorrie. We can't risk that there might be someone waiting to hurt you," he explained. "You shouldn't be seen down here. Plus, Sam knows you. He doesn't know Jason."

"If they're waiting to hurt me," I countered, "they would do the same to you."

"I agree with Chase," Jason chimed in, making me feel even more betrayed. "You should stay out of sight."

"But by that logic, so should Chase," I argued.

Chase shook his head. "The only reason to hurt me would be if I had information that you didn't know, and I don't. Attacking me would only make things *more* obvious to you."

I shook my head in return. I was out of arguments. I could have said that as a vampire, Jason shouldn't be seen in the underground either, but I didn't want Chase running around in the dark alone.

"Fine," I said finally, "but you guys better not keep me waiting here all night. I'll call you if Sam shows up."

With a final nod, they both left me in the creepy dark room by myself. Feeling useless as the door shut behind them, I slumped to the ground and sat with my knees pulled up to my chest.

"I thought they'd never leave," came a voice from out of the darkness.

I hopped to my feet and looked around the room. At first I saw nothing out of the ordinary, then the shadowy shapes I'd seen before shimmered into being and began darting along the walls from a central point. As the last of the shapes left the center, Sam appeared.

"They were hiding you," I breathed as I tried to calm my pulse. "Why?"

"Because I'm going to help you find your father," he explained, "and your two escorts would have stood in the way."

"Why would you help me now and not before?" I asked sharply.

Sam smiled sadly. "Some new information recently came to light."

"That doesn't explain anything," I replied.

"It doesn't have to."

I didn't understand the morose look on Sam's face, but I knew I didn't like it. Still, I wanted to find my dad.

"What did you have in mind?" I asked finally.

Sam glanced nervously at the door, as if someone might burst in at any moment. "The witches are trying to summon another demon," he explained. "I could help you to jump in and get summoned as well."

I inhaled sharply in surprise. "But wouldn't that just leave me in the same position as my dad?"

Sam glanced at the door again. "You're half-human. The witches will have taken precautions against demon blood, which is why they could hold your dad, but their precautions won't work as well on you."

I shook my head, thinking about the wardings at Sasha's house that hadn't worked as intended. Maybe the witches were actually learning from their mistakes this time, but if so, they should have taken precautions against angry half-demons as well, since one was about to come their way.

"There isn't much time," Sam said nervously. "You must decide now."

It was my turn to glance at the door, wishing that I hadn't let Chase and Jason leave. Then again, Sam was right, they would have tried to stop me.

"You'll tell Chase and Jason where I went when they get back?" I asked hopefully.

Sam nodded. "Don't worry, I'll babysit them for as long as you need."

I took a step toward Sam. "Do it."

Sam closed his eyes and lifted both of his arms above his head dramatically. The shadowy shapes that had settled into the dark crevices of the room suddenly surged forward. They flowed around Sam's still form and poured toward me. My instincts screamed at me to run, and it took everything I had to stand in place. I was overcome with an electric feeling as they hit me and started swirling around my body in a dizzying mass. It almost tickled where the some of the shapes touched me, but others made my skin burn.

As the shapes closed in enough that I could no longer see Sam, I had a feeling of moving upward, almost like what I felt when I made a portal, but instead of simply popping into being somewhere else, it felt like I was dissolving. I screamed, thinking it had all been a horrible trick and Sam had betrayed me, but my scream was cut short as my body dissolved into nothing.

There was a moment of blackness, where all I could think was that I was dead, then I could feel my face and my heartbeat. Ever so slowly, the feeling of having a torso and limbs returned to me.

I was in a dark, stone room that felt oddly familiar. I sat up with a gasp as the bars across the front of the room came into view. What looked like candlelight flickered off the cool metal. I knew just where I was, and it was a place I had never hoped to return to. Memories of escaping that same room with Allison, Lela, and Brian came flooding back.

The steel bars that looked slightly dingy now had been installed by the group of witches who had kidnapped us. I had assumed that my dad had gotten rid of the bars when he covered up all that happened, but I guess not. The cell was in one of the old-style crypts underneath Shelby's cemetery. The crypts had all been sealed, until the witches decided to take this one over.

As I watched, several faces came into view as people peeked around the corner through the bars. I thought I recognized several of them, but upon seeing me they quickly withdrew.

"It's the demon girl," I heard one say. "It worked."

"What do you mean, *it worked*?" I asked, using annoyance to cover up my fear.

"Our part in this is almost over," another said, though they weren't speaking to me.

Confused, I thought over what Sam had said. He'd claimed that they were trying to summon some other demon, but that I could hop in in that demon's place. Yet, the witches were expecting me.

"What *worked*?" I asked again sharply, but all I could hear was the sound of retreating footsteps, leaving me alone in the near darkness.

Panicking, I thought of my dad's house and tried to make a portal, but nothing happened. Next I tried to summon a flame into my hand. Nothing. If the witches were specifically trying to summon me, then Sam must have known. He betrayed me, but why? As far as I knew, they could summon me without help, at least as far as traditional summonings were concerned. Then it dawned on me that the reason the witches were able to summon demons entirely wasn't because they had discovered some new magic, it was because they had help. Somehow Sam used his spectral henchmen to carry demons fully to the human world. Sam had been the last person my father talked to, right before being summoned himself.

I punched the wall before I could think about it, and my knuckles came away bloody. Rage like I hadn't felt in what seemed like quite a while boiled in the pit of my stomach, and the small, stinging pain in my knuckles wasn't enough to dampen it. Normally that type of rage meant I would be blowing things up, but nothing was happening. My magic had somehow been nullified. With a cry of anger, I side-kicked at the bars, then nearly fell as the bars bent under my foot.

I didn't take the time to be surprised. I knew I was capable of supernatural strength, but it had happened to me so rarely that I never really thought about it. With another cry of rage I threw my whole body against the bars. The impact rattled my bones, but the pain of the impact only spurred me on more.

I threw my body against the bars over and over, until finally several of the bars broke loose from where they'd been cemented into the ground. Shaking violently, I wiggled the bars loose and slipped out of the cell.

I knew that I'd made a lot of noise, and the witches

would probably be rushing to contain me, so I had to be quick. I rushed toward the stairs, but was stopped by the sound of a single pair of high-heels clicking down the stone surface. Wanting to surprise whoever it was, I hid in the darkness beside the foot of the stairs, ready to pounce.

First a pair of green, high-heeled boots came into view, followed by the edges of an emerald green trench coat.

"You?" I said, so stunned that I forgot about the element of surprise. "What are *you* doing here?"

My grandmother's smiling face came into view. "I'll need you to return to your cell, Alexondra."

Tears welled up in my eyes when I realized that not only was she not there to save me, she had been the one who wanted me captured.

"Why?" I asked, too shocked to move.

"I had no choice," she said almost sadly.

A groan from the cell beside the one I'd been summoned into distracted me. I'd assumed it was empty, and had been too panicked to think of checking it out. My grandmother's green eyes darted over to the cell, then back to my face. It was only the third time I'd laid eyes upon her, and I was once again startled to realize how much she looked like me, or how much, I guess, I looked like her.

"Xoe?" someone mumbled from the cell, then more frantically, "Xoe! Get out of here *now*!"

"Dad?" I asked weakly. I wanted to rush over to the

cell, but I wasn't about to turn my back on grandmother dearest.

I watched out of the corner of my eye as his shape stumbled into view to lean against the bars of his cell. The small amount of light in the crypt hit his face. He looked ghostly pale and weak, even though he had only been missing for a day.

"Run," he pleaded. "She's going to hurt you. Run!" The final shout seemed to take all of the strength out of him, and he crumpled back to the ground.

I began to pant as rage washed up in me once again. I looked up into my grandmother's young, smiling face and knew in that moment that if I had my magic I would have tried to kill her. Opting for the second best option, I swung my fist and connected with her jaw, sending her rocking backwards.

I went after her, intent on at least incapacitating her, but she poofed out of my grasp in a whoosh of green smoke. Apparently whatever kept me from using magic wasn't set up to affect her. Her form re-solidified inside my dad's cell, except now she was holding a long, thin sword in her right hand. I'd seen the sword before, when she'd decapitated Bartimus to save my life.

She pointed the sword down at my dad's prostrate form as she held up her other hand to touch her jaw where I'd hit her. "Back in your cell now, Alexandra, or you will be halfway to becoming an orphan."

"He's your son," I said shakily, not believing that she would actually hurt him.

"Don't do it, Xoe," my dad pleaded weakly. "*Run.*"

"We can all walk out of here *alive*, Alexondra," my grandmother interrupted.

"She's lying," my dad said, but was cut off as my grandmother prodded him with her blade.

"Tell me the truth," I said calmly, "and I will get back in my cell."

My grandmother sighed, then poofed back out to stand beside me. "I've been alive a very long time," she explained, as if it explained anything, "and I've made many enemies."

"You're making another one right now," I commented, unable to help myself.

She looked at me sharply, then continued. "They would have killed me already, except I've grown quite adept at hiding," she went on. "I'm *tired* of hiding, but I had no way out, you see?"

Realizing that she expected me to answer, I shook my head. "No, I don't see."

My grandmother sighed and flipped her long, blonde hair over the shoulder of her green trench coat. "When I first discovered that your powers were so close to mine," she said as she looked down at me, "I didn't think much of it. As I've told you before, demons have no need for family."

"Then why did you save me from Bart?" I asked numbly.

My grandmother's face was expressionless as she said, "Because I knew you could be useful, if only I could figure out *how* to use you. Then I thought of witches, and how useful they can be in large numbers."

She took a few steps closer to me. I tried to step away, but my back ended up against the stone wall opposite my dad's cell.

"Your powers are so similar to mine," she said distantly as she reached her left hand toward my face, "and you look so much like me. It wouldn't be much of a change at all."

"*What* are you talking about? I asked as I began to panic again. Having nowhere else to go, I backed away toward the cell I'd arrived in.

She sighed again. "You really are quite daft, aren't you? I want the witches to *switch* us. Normally they wouldn't be capable of such of feat on their own, but with my help it will work."

"Switch us?" I asked, still not understanding what she was getting at.

She marched toward me like an angry cat, swishing her hips from side to side with her long blade pointed at the ground. "I will be you, and you will be me. I'll have a nice, fresh start, and you can deal with my numerous pursuers."

I began to shake as my back hit another wall. "You have no intention of letting my father go," I accused. "He would never let you steal my life."

The look on her face let me know that she was right. After the witches *switched* us, she would kill my dad, and she would kill me. Heck, she would probably even kill the witches to avoid any loose ends.

She had almost reached me when I lunged at her. Getting back in my cell would do no good. My father would end up dead, and I probably wouldn't last much longer than him.

She poofed out of reach again, and back into my father's cell, only this time she stabbed her blade downward into his chest. I screamed, and she poofed back out beside me. I stared at my dad's still form, but it was too dark for me to see whether or not he was still breathing.

"Get. Back. In. Your. Cell," she said, emphasizing each word to sound like an angry parent, but she wasn't like any parent I'd ever known. She'd just stabbed her own son.

I felt like I might faint, but knew if I did it would be all over. I wouldn't be able to help my dad if I was unconscious. I swallowed the lump in my throat. *Please don't let it be too late to help him.*

Movement caught my eye and I looked down to see the ring on my finger flashing wildly with red light. My grandmother looked down at the ring, *her* ring, in surprise as it cast glowing red shapes across her pale face. I felt just as surprised as the feel of magic trickled down through my finger into my body. My magic might have been blocked, but the ring still had its own little store. Ignoring the bloody sword that she half-pointed toward me, I grabbed her right arm.

Energy pulsed up through my palm as she tried to poof away again, but something about my grip on her arm was preventing her. She looked at me slightly stunned, then dropped her sword and grabbed my wrist with her left arm. Something pulsed back and forth between us as I felt my magic somehow return to me. My grandmother's lips parted in surprise as we were lifted upwards into a portal. I tried to let go, but she had a firm grip on me.

"What are you doing!" she shouted over the sound of rushing wind.

"I'm not doing anything!" I shouted back.

The next thing I knew, we were crashing down into another place that I recognized. The night sky of the dream-world loomed over our heads, pushing down on us with invisible hands.

My grandmother pulled away from me and wiped her palms on her coat in irritation. "Bringing us to the dream-world won't help you escape, Alexondra. I know this world like the back of my hand."

I began to cry as I thought about my dad. "You stabbed him!" I screamed. "You stabbed your own son!"

She narrowed her eyes at me. "You gave me no choice."

"That's a lie!" I screamed back.

"I loved him in my own way!" she shouted back at me, "but I love *me* more."

I shook my head. "You aren't capable of loving *anything*."

She marched toward me again as rage coated her face. "*Why*," she demanded, "did you bring me here?"

"I didn't!" I cried.

Her face turned thoughtful as her anger dripped away. She began pacing while she thought about what I said. How could she be so cold about what she'd just done?

"It must have been our magics reacting with each other," she speculated, "how strange."

I fell to my knees as the full weight of what had transpired hit me.

"Why are you doing this?" I asked as tears covered my face.

My grandmother looked down on me like I was nothing more than a bothersome insect. "I saw an opportunity, and I took it. Did you know that those rogue wolves were planning on killing you? They probably would have succeeded too. Really, I'm doing you a favor by taking over your life. You were doing a horrible job of running it."

I took a deep, shaky breathe, but felt unable to get to my feet. "What do the rogue wolves have to do with any of this?" I rasped.

"Nothing," she snapped. "I caught word that the little group of witches in your town were *trying* to summon demons. In I popped, letting them think that they had summoned me. They wanted information on how to kill you, and thought that another demon was the best source. I took over from there."

"What about the other demon, the one who killed Claire and Sasha?" I asked. I considered creating a portal back to my dad, but she would only follow me. I had to finish this here. If only I didn't feel so weak.

She laughed. "That pesky little thing? I had to draw you out somehow. Couldn't have you moping in the underground forever."

"Why?" I said, confused. "Why bring me up at all when you could just use Sam to put me where you wanted me, just like you did my dad."

"I led your father to Sam with a tidbit of information," she explained, "but I had little chance of leading you. Although, the fact that you went to him *was* convenient. After your first visit, I knew you would likely go back, and things became simple from there."

It occurred to me that maybe my grandmother was a little bit afraid of me. Otherwise she would have just snatched me as soon as she thought of her plan. I wasn't sure what she saw that I didn't, because at that moment, my grandmother was the scariest thing I'd ever seen.

She came to crouch in front of me, and I almost thought that she would show sympathy, but suddenly her hand was around my neck and she was lifting me to my feet. She kept on lifting until my toes barely touched the ground.

"We're going back to the witches now," she explained. "I must finish what I started."

I tried to summon my magic to get her away from me, but nothing was happening. I couldn't burn her because of her demon aura, and she was too close for me to throw a fireball at her.

My vision began to go black, just as something came barreling into my grandmother's side. I fell out of her grasp and to the ground. At first I thought one of the many monster-like denizens of the dream-world had struck her, but then I saw the shining white skin and translucent hair.

The sparkly white figure rose up from where it had landed with my grandmother's still form several paces away.

"D-Dorrie?" I stammered, not believing my eyes.

Dorrie whipped her head around to face me with tears in her luminescent blue eyes, then looked back down at my grandmother. "I'm so sorry Pop Tart! I-I thought she was going to hurt you."

I stumbled to my feet and went to where Dorrie stood. I looked down at my grandmother's still form, her neck twisted at an awkward angle to the side. It seemed almost anticlimactic.

"I thought you were dead," I whispered numbly.

Dorrie shook her head. "Your granny came to visit and she went after me. I hid in the bathroom, and then everything went black. When I woke up, I was here."

I turned away from my grandmother's corpse, no longer able to look at it. I felt sort of like I was floating. "I saw your body," I explained. "You were shattered."

Dorrie smiled softly despite her tears. "I'm a construct of demon magic, made for a purpose. When I was hurt, I was remade where I was supposed to be, only I don't have a cab anymore. I've been waiting here ever since."

"I need to go," I said softly. Before I could form a portal, something knocked into me from behind. I stumbled forward, then turned back to my grandmother's corpse, fearing that she wasn't dead after all. Yet there she lay, just as still as before.

I shook my head, it had probably been one of the shadowy dream-world shapes that you could only ever really see out of the corner of your eyes. I thought of the crypt where I'd left my dad, hoping I wasn't too late. I *couldn't* be too late. Before I could could escape, Dorrie grabbed my hand. I looked down at our joined hands to see the ring flashing wildly again. To my surprise, instead of the disorienting feel of traveling through a portal, Dorrie and I both dissipated in a whoosh of red smoke. Somehow I'd finally figured out the same trick that both my dad and grandmother used to travel.

The same red smoke led the way as we reappeared back underneath the cemetery. The crypt was silent as we reached it, and my dad was very, *very* still. Dorrie used her inhuman strength to pry apart the bars of his cell effortlessly, and I rushed inside. I crouched down and turned my dad's still form over so I could see his face. Lifeless, green eyes stared back at me.

I felt like my insides were being torn apart as I looked at my dad's dead gaze. I collapsed on top of him, and felt his cooling blood soak into my shirt. It was *my* fault. It was up to me to save him and I'd been tricked by Sam like an idiot.

Dorrie's rough hands pulled me away from my dad's body. She hugged me to her chest as we both cried. Sam had done this. I couldn't just sit there and feel this horrible, tearing feeling inside me. Sam had to pay.

I pulled away from Dorrie, and knew that my face looked as numb as I suddenly felt. I peered past Dorrie as a young girl came into view. She had short, red hair, and appeared to be around 13 or 14.

"You must be Rose," I said softly. Tears continued to stream down my face, but I'd blocked out the pain of what had happened. I couldn't feel it. Not yet.

"P-please," Rose stammered. "The other witches left me here. I don't blame you for hurting Sasha. She should have never summoned demons."

I laughed, then abruptly cut myself short. Pretty sure that I was going into shock, I asked, "They told you that I was the one who killed Sasha?"

Rose cringed at the word *killed*. "Please, she said again. You already killed my sister. My parents can't lose another daughter."

"I didn't kill your sister," I snapped. After all they'd done to me, those witches had some nerve trying to pin murders on me just to cover their own tails. They deserved whatever they got.

"I wasn't the demon who killed your sister, or Sasha," I said with an almost cruel smile. "In fact, I don't know which demon did it, and as of this moment, I don't care.

The only advice I can give to you and your parents is to run, and keep running, because I'm not going to help you. Part of me hopes that *you* will escape, but I hope all of the others are torn to shreds."

Rose started crying as she collapsed to her knees. I knew I should care more about her fate, but I just couldn't. I couldn't care anymore about anything.

Rose's eyes moved to take in the entire scene. "Was that your dad?" she asked weakly.

I froze. I couldn't look down at him again . . . but I *had* to. There was no way I was leaving his body down in that crypt. I stood and took a few steps back, gesturing for Dorrie to do the same.

I closed my eyes and with a single thought, my dad's body went up in flames. Normally I could only throw fire at a demon. I couldn't burn them or set fire to them directly because their demon aura protected them. It was the final test. As I looked down at the burning form, I knew that he really was gone.

I glanced over to see that Rose had pushed her back against the wall, but hadn't tried to run. It occurred to me that she was too panicked to try. She was just a kid. I hadn't felt like a kid in a very long time. I stared at her until her eyes met mine.

"Tell your parents to call me if they figure out where the demon went to," I ordered.

Rose's tear-stained face scrunched up in confusion. "I thought you said you weren't going to help us."

I shook my head, almost regretting offering at all . . .

but she was just a kid. Not every teenager deserved to have a life as screwed up as mine. "I'll help *you*, but that's it. The demon can kill all of the others."

Rose just stared at me, too shocked to say anything else. I turned away from her frightened eyes and held out a hand to Dorrie. I suddenly knew exactly how to get to where I needed to go without a portal, and couldn't believe that I hadn't figured it out until then. We dissipated once more in a puff of red smoke.

As soon as my feet were solidly on the ground, I pulled away from Dorrie. Chase, Jason, and Sam all sat together on the floor like nothing was wrong. Blinded by rage like I had never felt before, I charged toward Sam and slammed into him, sending us both to the ground. If I had thought of it, I would have thrown a fireball at him, but I wasn't thinking. All of the numbness I'd felt in the crypt was gone. I straddled him and began throttling his face, oblivious to the pain as my knuckles split open from the repeated impact.

Arms lifted me away and I screamed. The arms on one side dropped me only to be replaced by Dorrie's rough hands. Suddenly I broke down and went limp. I ended up on the ground with Chase's arms around me to keep me still as Jason came to crouch in front of me. His crouch was awkward, drawing me to the fact that the skin of his palms where he'd gripped me was blackened and peeling. I'd nearly burned his hands off when he tried to pull me away from Sam. Chase was only saved because of his demon blood.

Dorrie smiled at Chase, and I realized that he had probably been staring at her in shock that she was alive, but I couldn't see his face with his arms wrapped around me, so I didn't know for sure.

"What happened Xoe?" Jason asked as he looked at me with wide eyes, but I couldn't speak to answer him.

I turned my blank stare back to Dorrie.

"Her father," Dorrie began, but her voice cracked.

"My father is dead," I said, feeling numb once again.

Chase's arms went very still as Jason looked at me in shock.

"I didn't know she wanted to hurt you," Sam said from somewhere out of my sight, referring to my grandmother. "I would have never helped had I known. I swear it."

"What?" Chase asked. I felt his arms pull away as he stood to look at his brother. "Sam, what did you do?"

"The spirits only told me what happened after it was already occurring," Sam said in a pleading tone.

I turned as Chase took a menacing step toward his brother. Sam held up his hands in a defensive gesture as his nose steadily dripped blood from my throttling.

"I didn't know," he said quickly. "I swear I didn't know. It was too late to save her dad, and Xoe had already disappeared to the dream-world. We wouldn't have been able to reach her."

"You just sat here," Chase began like it pained him to speak, "knowing what was happening, and you said nothing? What if Xoe had been killed? Would you have even told us what happened?"

"No," Sam said honestly.

Chase clenched and unclenched his fists like he was considering using them on his brother. "You were hoping Xoe would die, weren't you? That way no one would have known what happened. No loose ends."

Sam stared back at him, unable to dispute the claims against him.

Everyone was silent while Chase made his decision. "Get out of here, Sam," he said finally, "or next time we won't pull her off of you."

I buried my head in my hands as the sounds of Sam scuttling to his feet and making his escape echoed through the small space. Suddenly I felt Chase's hand on my shoulder as he sat down beside me. When I didn't move away, he wrapped an arm around me.

"She wanted to take over my life," I said in a shaky voice. "She said too many demons were after her, so she wanted to have the witches switch us so I could get chased instead. My dad told me to run, but I-I couldn't."

"She's talking about her granny," Dorrie explained softly. Chase and Jason must have looked confused, but I still hadn't lifted my head from my hands long enough to see them.

Chase stroked my hair as I cried, not asking for any more of an explanation. I glanced up to see Jason's lost expression as his hands hovered over me, wanting to touch me, but unable to with his burns. Then I buried my face in Chase's chest and cried. I could hear Dorrie softly elaborating on my explanation, but I did my best to shut out her voice.

Eventually Chase stood and lifted me up into his arms. Everyone was silent as we left the little room. I didn't know where we were going, and I didn't care. Exhaustion took me while I was in Chase's arms and I fell into a deep, black sleep.

12

————

I awoke in my room at my dad's house. *My dad*. I felt too tired to cry as I sat up and looked around the barren room. I hadn't done much with it, as I'd been too depressed after being kicked out of my mom's house. I closed my eyes and thought of where I really wanted to be, knowing that I wouldn't destroy the room I was leaving.

I appeared in my mom's living room, startling her so much that she spilled her morning coffee all over the couch as the red smoke around me faded. I found myself wishing that my smoke was gray like my dad's had been, but at least it wasn't green like my grandmother's. I don't think I would have been able to handle that.

"X-Xoe?" she questioned as she waved her coffee-burned hand in the air.

I just looked at her, letting her see everything that I was feeling, and suddenly she stood and wrapped me in her arms without a word. I began to cry while my mom made comforting hushing noises in my ear and stroked my hair.

We sat down on the couch, and I was able to steady my breathing enough to tell her what happened. I told her *everything*, forcing myself to relive the horrible scene with my dad and my grandmother. I was half an orphan now, just like my grandmother had said.

My mom began to cry too as she hugged me again, and we cried until there was nothing left of either of us.

Eventually I sat up.

"Xoe," my mom said before I could say anything. "I didn't ask you to leave because I was afraid of you. I asked you to leave because I was afraid *for* you."

I turned to look at her, but didn't reply.

She took a deep breath. "I felt so ashamed that I was incapable of protecting you. That was supposed to be my job, and I failed. I thought you would be better off with your father, with someone who knew how to keep you safe. I didn't deserve to have you."

My mouth fell open in shock, just when I thought that nothing else would ever shock me again. "I thought you hated me for destroying your house," I said softly.

My mom's face crumpled. "I could never hate you, Xoe. I was just so afraid of something happening, something that I wouldn't be able to save you from."

I nodded as it all sunk in. "I have to go," I mumbled eventually.

My mom sat up too, and looked at me with eyes

almost too puffy to see out of. "Don't Xoe. You should move back here. *Please*."

I nodded again as relief flooded me, but what I said was, "I mean, I have to go because I left Jason stranded in the demon underground."

My mom inhaled sharply and nodded. "O-oh. I understand. Just come back here as soon as you get him, okay?"

I nodded and stood, then went out the front door. Just because I knew I wouldn't destroy anything, didn't mean I should keep taking chances. I went out into the yard, then pictured my dad's house. Red smoke surrounded me, and I was gone.

I popped silently into the kitchen to find Chase, Jason, and Dorrie discussing where I might have gone. As soon as they saw me, they all rushed forward, their worry palpable.

"I just thought Jason might want to go back up," I mumbled, ignoring their worried faces as they fawned over me.

Jason stepped back in surprise, then nodded and said, "Okay."

I reached out a hand to him as I turned my head to look at Chase. "Do you want to stay here with Dorrie?" I asked.

"Where are you going to go?" he asked instead of answering me.

"To my mom's," I answered without emotion.

Everyone paused for a moment, then Chase nodded and took a step back. "I understand."

I wasn't sure what he meant. Did he understand that I just needed to be alone? That I needed to be in my own bed, somewhere I felt even slightly normal? I hoped so. I gripped Jason's hand in mine, then suddenly we were on my mom's front porch.

Jason's right hand was still entwined with mine as we stood looking at my mom's house. He looked at me as his left hand reached forward to stroke my hair, but I pulled away.

"Maybe I should actually go away this time," he said barely above a whisper as he let his hand drop, "but I don't think I can."

I looked at him sadly, and knew that all of the pain I was feeling was clear on my face. Everything was going to change.

Jason reached out to touch my hair again, and this time I let him. "I'm not going to hold you back from whatever it is that might make you happy. I know right now that it's not me."

I opened my mouth to argue, then closed it. After a minute more I said, "I don't know if I'll ever be happy again. I can't even think about it right now."

"And I'll be your friend until you figure it out," Jason said softly.

"My friend?" I asked, not sure I could take any more loss, but knowing that it was the right thing to do.

"Is that what you want?" he asked instead of answering.

I nodded in reply. I knew things would never be that simple. That one day you could be in love, and the next you could just be friends, friends that were maybe still in love. Yet I also knew that Jason wasn't what I needed right then.

We stood in silence with our hands still entwined for a long while until my mom came out to gather me. She put an arm around me and walked me inside, leaving Jason alone on the porch.

It was still morning, but I felt almost too tired to stand. Somehow understanding my plight, my mom walked me upstairs to my old bedroom. The room was exactly how I'd left it, minus the destruction I'd caused with my portal. I crawled into my bed, and my mom sat beside me as I fell asleep.

That was where I stayed for several days. My mom coaxed me into eating, but it was a struggle. I felt numb and hollow. I heard the doorbell ring periodically downstairs, and I listened as my mom turned my friends away at my request. On two different occasions Devin and Abel showed up, and my mom turned them away just the same.

Jason visited every day, and he my mom let inside, though she didn't let him upstairs. I listened as they talked in hushed whispers, only able to make out a word here or there.

On the night of the third day I finally dreamed, unlike the dreams of pure blackness I'd had the previous nights.

I was in the dream-world, but I could tell that I wasn't physically there. My dad was sitting on the bench at the bus stop, looking at his expensive watch. I went and sat beside him, then looked at him expectantly.

"These cursed cabs are never on time," he commented as he looked out at the road.

I felt a few tears slip down my face. "What are you doing here, dad?"

He looked down at me warmly. "Are you happy, Xoe?"

I shook my head. "No."

"Why not?" he asked, perplexed.

"You're dead," I choked out.

My dad chuckled. "We've known each other for such a short time. Surely your happiness cannot be so dependent on me?"

"You were a big part of it," I admitted.

My dad put an arm around me. "You'll simply have to go after the other parts of it, to make up for what's lacking."

I shook my head and took in a shaky breath. "I don't know how."

My dad snorted. "*Please*. My daughter cannot be defeated by something so trivial. You've much to do with your life."

"Like what?" I questioned. As far as I could see, my life didn't have much purpose at all.

"Do what makes you happy. That's all you can ever really do." He stood as a cab finally approached.

"Don't go," I begged as he began to walk away.

He turned and smiled at me. "I'm already gone."

With that he got into the cab and drove away, leaving me to cry on the bench alone.

The sun shining through my window was blindingly bright as I startled into awareness. I sat up and put my feet on the ground, feeling stiff from having spent so much time in bed.

I rose and left my room to walk downstairs to an empty house. I vaguely remembered my mom telling me she had to go back to work that day. With my stomach growling, I went to make coffee in a mechanical manner, one step after another.

I had just poured myself a cup when someone knocked on the door. My mind raced with the possibilities of who it could be. I covertly peeked out of the kitchen window in an attempt to see whoever it was without them seeing me, but Devin spotted me instantly. Surprisingly, he was alone. The other two times he'd come, Abel had been with him.

"I see you Xoe!" he called. "Open the door."

Too tired and apathetic to argue, I left the kitchen and did as he asked. We stood face to face for a moment as I took in his neatly combed blond hair, freshly shaven face, light blue button up that matched his eyes, and gray slacks. He raised an eyebrow at my appearance, then gestured for me to come out onto the porch.

Not caring that I was in dingy, and probably smelly, pajamas, I followed Devin to sit on the swinging bench that dominated a good portion of the porch. The hard wood of the bench felt more uncomfortable than normal on my stiff joints and muscles. Lying in bed for several days definitely didn't do a body good.

We swung gently back and forth in silence for a few minutes while I sipped my coffee, until finally he cleared his throat to speak. "My father died when I was sixteen," he said.

I froze and kept my gaze firmly in front of me. "Please," I pleaded, "I can't talk about this yet."

"You don't have to talk," he consoled, "but you do need to listen."

I didn't say anything in reply, and instead just sipped my coffee.

"My parents were both werewolves," he began again, "so I was born with the affliction, though I didn't start turning until I was a teenager. We were all rogues, without a pack or protection," he said without emotion. "We didn't understand what the coalition could offer, and so we thought that they only sought to control.

"Eventually another rogue wolf found us, someone like Dan who wanted to make a pack of his own, outside of the coalition. He wanted my mother and I, and so he tried to take us. If my dad would have just let us go, he would have lived, but he tried to protect us. The other wolf ripped my dad's heart out of his chest while I watched," he finished.

I inhaled sharply, surprised at the sudden turn in the story. Images flashed through my head of my own dad's death. I had been right there. I could have stopped it.

"I couldn't have stopped it," Devin said, as if reading my thoughts. "I didn't think that the other wolf would really hurt him . . . and then it was too late."

We sat in silence for several minutes while I looked down at my coffee. It was a beautiful, clear day outside, and I felt almost like it was mocking me.

"I'm guessing Jason told you what happened," I said bitterly.

Devin nodded, but didn't reply.

"I could have stopped her," I admitted. "I didn't think she'd actually hurt him, but I should have known. I should never have put any faith in a woman I'd only just met, family ties or not."

Devin sighed. "What would your father have wanted you to do in that moment?"

I shook my head as I began to cry. It seemed like I should have been out of tears after all that I'd shed, but they just kept on coming. "He wanted me to run."

"And why didn't you?"

I shook my head again, not understanding where he was going with this. "I couldn't just *leave* him there."

"When the wolf came after my family," he began, "my father held him off. He told me to run . . . and I tried. The only thing that kept me in that house was the other wolf throwing me into a wall so hard that I was too stunned to walk. After my father was dead, I ran while my mom held the wolf off."

"It wasn't your fault," I consoled automatically. "You were just a kid, and your parents were trying to protect you. If you had been hurt or taken, their efforts would have been in vain."

"Xoe," he began again shaking his head. "*You're* just a kid, and your dad was trying to protect you."

My head started throbbing as I felt guilty for a whole other reason. My dad's last wish had been for me to run, and I had been too selfish to grant it. "I couldn't even let him do the thing he gave his life for," I sighed.

Devin put a hand on my shoulder. "*Xoe*, do you understand what I would give to go back in time and tear my father's murderer to shreds?"

I stifled a shiver. "I didn't kill my grandmother, my friend did. Even then, it was an accident."

"But you would have," he prompted. "You didn't try to save your own hide after your dad gave his life. You didn't just let his killer go."

I thought about what he said, and knew he was right. Grandmother or no, I would have killed her. She had betrayed her own son. She deserved to die.

"What happened next?" I asked, referring to his story.

Devin smiled distantly, understanding my meaning. "I went to the coalition. I'd hoped that they could help me find the wolf who'd killed my father. Abel's father was still the coalition head at that point. He did all that he could, but I never got my revenge. After a few weeks I tried to leave, but he said he couldn't let me. Everything my parents had told me came rushing back, that the coalition only sought to control.

"I told him I could never be part of a pack, that I found the idea detestable. It was the idea of a pack that took my parents away from me."

"But you're not part of a pack now," I interrupted.

When I'd first met Devin he had explained to me that he served as a kind of advisor for Abel. He was affiliated with the coalition, but didn't answer to a pack leader, nor did he lead his own pack.

"And I never have been," he explained. "Abel's father let me work for the coalition without joining a pack. That way I was accounted for, and felt no need to run away. Though really, I had nowhere else to go. Abel and I became friends, and when he took over I was able to maintain my position."

I nodded and stared off at the trees. I suddenly had a much different perspective on Devin.

"It's okay to mourn," he continued when I didn't speak, "but don't blame yourself. You are more brave than any seventeen year-old I've ever met. You're more brave than me."

We sat in silence for several more minutes while I thought over what he'd said. I didn't feel brave. I felt stupid. I felt like I should have figured out what was going on sooner.

"I don't know what to do now. I don't know how to move on," I admitted.

Devin smiled softly. "What would your dad want you to do?"

"He wants me to be happy," I replied, remembering my dream.

"Then do it," Devin stated.

I shook my head. "I can't."

Devin poked me in the arm, demanding my full attention. "You run your own werewolf pack, you've defeated witches, vampires, and ancient demons. You've proven that *can't* isn't in your vocabulary."

I stared down at my mug of half-full, cold, coffee. "I don't know where to start."

Devin took the mug of coffee from me and set in on the porch. "You pick something that is under your control," he explained, "something that makes your life *better*. Then you take it or you do it, whatever it is."

My dad's words echoed in my head, *Do what makes you happy. That's all you can ever really do.*

I stood. "There's somewhere I need to go."

Devin stood as well and gave me a light punch on the arm. "There she is!"

I couldn't help my small smile, the first smile that had come to my face in days. It felt odd that Devin had been the one to bring it on, but I was also grateful. I walked back toward my front door, but something stopped me. Looking back over my shoulder at Devin I asked, "What happened to your mom?"

He met my eyes squarely. "I never found her."

I shook my head. My heart would have ached for him if it wasn't already broken. "Don't give up," I said softly.

Devin smiled bitterly. "It's been twelve years. She is lost to me."

"*Don't* give up," I demanded again.

Devin looked at me thoughtfully for a moment before nodding and saying, "Okay."

I really wanted to take a shower, but another thought stopped me. "The rogue wolves wanted to kill me. That's why they contacted the witches."

Devin smiled. "We found a few of the witches who spilled the beans. We're taking care of it."

"Is my mom safe? And my friends?"

Devin nodded. "We won't leave until we're sure the threat has been eliminated."

With that I went back inside to shower and get dressed. I had somewhere to be.

13

_____

Chase was in his room reading when I found him. It was strange to be back in my dad's house, but I knew it was something I had to face. I couldn't just leave Chase and Dorrie stranded down there forever.

"Xoe!" he exclaimed, startled by my sudden appearance.

He put his book down on the bed as he stood, then rushed over to me. He put his hands gently on my arms and searched my face for some clue as to how I was feeling.

"Hi," I said weakly, not knowing what else to say.

His face fell a little at my lackluster reply. "I thought you might never come back," he admitted. "Though I see you've learned to travel without a portal. I thought maybe I just imagined the smoke when you came for Jason."

I looked into his earnest gray eyes for a moment more,

then pulled him in for a hug. I let out a shaky breath as he put his arms around me. I was still so very tired. After several minutes, he lifted me up and carried me over to his bed where he set me down so we could sit side by side.

He handed me a manilla file folder that I hadn't noticed sitting on his bed. I looked a question at him, and he gestured for me to look inside.

I opened the folder to the first page to find information on my grandmother. I went to slam the folder shut, but Chase gently gripped my wrist and helped me move the first sheet to look at the next page. The next page was on . . . me.

My lips formed a soft "o" of surprise as I began to read the typed information. There was even a list of my powers compared to my grandmother's powers, and the powers of someone named Art.

"This folder was on our doorstep yesterday," Chase explained. "I imagine Sam left it. I tried to track him down for an explanation, but he's cleaned up shop. I can't find him anywhere."

My breath hitched a little at the thought of Sam. I vaguely remembered pummeling him, but it had all seemed like a dream. He'd claimed that he didn't know he was endangering me or my father, but a person might claim a lot of things when faced with someone ready to kill him.

"What does it all mean?" I asked numbly.

Chase shook his head. "I don't know. I think your dad

was researching your powers, and comparing them to those of your ancestors. I'm guessing the other person listed, Art, is related to you in some way."

"My grandmother said she led my dad to Sam. She somehow made him think that this information was important. Important enough that he was running around trying to figure it out without letting me know."

Chase nodded. "There was something else going on. I've wracked my brain trying to figure out what it was, but I'm still not sure. I think the only reason he let us get involved with the witches was to keep us busy. He probably thought that they were harmless."

I closed the folder and set it behind me on the bed. I knew my father had been trying to protect me from something, but from what? He obviously didn't know that my grandmother was a threat, or he would never have listened to her. He wouldn't have gone to Sam based on whatever information she told him. Yet, I didn't see what my powers and the powers of my ancestors had to do with anything.

I looked over at Chase as he cast his eyes downward. He looked tired, and his eyes were puffy. I reached out and ran a hand through his near-black hair to get his attention.

"I saw my dad in a dream last night," I said, ignoring the terrifying, falling feeling in the pit of my stomach.

"You did?" he asked almost hopefully.

I smiled, and for a moment felt almost normal as I said, "He told me to do what makes me happy."

"And what is that?" Chase asked as if honestly confused.

I leaned my head against his shoulder. "This, I think."

He tried to turn and look at me, but couldn't because of the angle, so I lifted my head back up. "Xoe-" he began in earnest.

I pressed my lips to his, cutting off whatever he'd wanted to say. There was a moment of frozen hesitation from Chase, then he gave in and kissed me back.

I pulled away slowly and smiled up at him, satisfied.

"I don't understand," he began, confused.

"I just needed to do that," I replied, "because what I have to say now is hard to explain."

Chase looked nervous, but nodded for me to go on.

"Jason and I have decided to be just friends," I began, "and when I first came here, I was planning on running right into your arms."

"But," Chase said for me.

"But," I repeated. "I don't think I'm ready for that. I think I need to figure out who I am now, after all that has happened. I need to figure out what I want to do without considering anyone else's feelings. I need to get my life together."

"You're allowed to not do anything for a while, Xoe," he said softly, turning away from me to gaze back down at the carpet.

I put a hand on the far side of his chin and turned him to face me. "I'm also allowed to move on with my life.

I think I want to do that with you, but I need to do it with myself first."

Chase stared at me for several heartbeats, then put both of his hands delicately on either side of my face and pulled me in to kiss him again. While exhilarating, the kiss was also comforting. It felt like *home,* a concept that had become strange and elusive to me as of late.

We ended the kiss and Chase looked steadily into my eyes. "I just needed one more," he explained with a smile. "Since I don't know if or when I'll be getting another."

I smiled back, glad he understood.

He let out a long sigh as he stretched his arms over his head, relieving the tension of the moment. "So what about the demon that's still running loose above-ground."

Recalling what I'd said to Rose, I felt a little sick. If she or her parents called, I would be there to help them, but the others could run for the rest of their lives for all I cared. "Knowing my luck, he'll show up and try to kill me someday soon," I joked.

"Why would he try to kill *you*?" Chase asked, perplexed.

I laughed again, feeling tired and comfortable enough that I knew if I laid back I would drift off to sleep.

"Well," I replied with a yawn, "all of the cool kids are doing it. He may as well give it a go."

"I haven't tried to kill you yet," he joked. "Does that mean I'm not a cool kid?"

I snorted. "Stick with me kid, and that's bound to change."

I gave in and laid back on the bed. There was still a painful, gaping wound in my heart left by my dad, but at that moment, it felt perhaps a little bit smaller. Eventually it would close up altogether, but I would always have the scar-tissue to remember him by.

14

Chase stayed underground with Dorrie when I went back to my mom's. It was a relief to have a new mode of travel, so I could pop back down and visit them whenever I wanted, and I could bring Chase up as he chose.

We were no closer to figuring out what to do about Dorrie. She had accidentally found her way back to the dream-world, but without a cab, she would have been stuck. For the time being she would just have to stay at my dad's house. She didn't seem upset about it, especially when I promised to visit her on a regular basis.

Devin and Abel are pretty sure that they've "eliminated" all of the rogue wolves, but they're staying in town for a while just to make sure. There have been talks about moving my pack to be combined with another larger pack, or else moving more wolves out to Shelby. The idea is safety in numbers, and I can't say that I disagree.

When the question of who would lead the new, larger pack came up, Abel insisted that I keep the job. I would have liked to argue, but he wasn't willing to let all of the work he put into making me a pack leader go to waste. He still wanted a demon connected to the coalition, and I had grudgingly began caring about all of them, not just my friends. Keeping the coalition safe meant that they would always be available to keep my friends safe.

Part of me hopes that Abel can find some wolves to move up here to keep things simple, but another part of me wouldn't mind eventually escaping Shelby. For the time being though, I'm happy to live back at my mom's.

I've seen Jason a few times, and he's upheld his promise to be my friend, though I've been avoiding being completely alone with him. He hasn't asked if I'm with Chase, but Lucy or Allison have probably already told him the answer that I gave to them:

Are you with Jason? No. Are you with Chase? Also, no. Well then who are you with? Myself.

Lucy and Allison think I'm just too afraid to make a real decision. Max thinks I'm, *"playing the field" as any self-respecting half-demon in her prime should do*. He got a withering look from Allison for that one.

As for me, I'm really not sure *what* I'm doing, but I know that it's the best thing for me. The only real problem on the horizon is the demon who killed Claire and Sasha, but I imagine he or she will show up eventually. I'm still coping with my grief, but with the help of my mom and my friends, it gets a little easier every day.

For the time being I'm just going to study for my GED, and try living as normal a life as I can. What could possibly go wrong?

Don't answer that.

ABOUT THE AUTHOR

For more information please visit www.saracroethle.com!

SNEAK PEEK AT BOOK SIX!

I placed the final clean dish into the dryer rack, then looked down at the dirty, soapy water in the sink. While I was glad to be living with my mom again, I wasn't thrilled to be back doing chores . . . especially now that the dishwasher decided to break.

I looked out my large kitchen window to the melting snow. The chilly Oregon winter had lasted long into spring, but it seemed it was finally letting up as sunlight danced across the ice in an almost dizzying display.

I glanced at the clock on the kitchen wall. Almost 9 am. Abel and Devin would arrive soon with our new pack members. Over the past six weeks, the decision had been made that instead of uprooting our small pack to join with a larger one, several other wolves would uproot their lives to join us. We were starting out with just two, but more would eventually come as each new person settled in. I had grudgingly accepted that I would still have to remain Alpha of the pack, since Abel believed having a demon in charge made us less likely to be attacked.

I wasn't sure I agreed with his logic. My presence hadn't stopped a group of rogue wolves from enlisting witches with the intent of wiping out my pack, less than two months before. I could finally admit that the witches had been mostly innocent, since they were only trying to stay alive, but their actions still led to my dad's death. Sure, my grandmother was really to blame, but she was dead. I needed someone of the living variety to be angry at, and the witches fit into that role nicely.

Of course, I hadn't seen any of them since I'd set fire to my father's corpse and returned to the demon underworld. They were all on the run from a demon they had foolishly summoned. Said demon had some sort of vendetta against them, and had already killed the coven's head witch, as well as the daughter of two coven members. If I crossed paths with the demon, I might try to send the fiend back underground, but I wasn't about to go out of my way to do anything concerning the witches.

I was pondering what type of demon the witches might be dealing with, when something hit the back of my head and kept pushing, shoving my face into the dishwater. The lukewarm water engulfed my entire head as the mini-wave created by my impact splashed down my chest. At first I was too surprised to act, but as whatever it was continued to hold me under, I began to thrash about, desperately seeking oxygen. Panicking, I braced my arms against the sink and kicked backward, but there was nothing there. I tried to use my sometimes supernatural strength to push myself away from the sink, yet whatever held me was incredibly strong and I didn't gain any ground.

As I struggled for a better grip on the counter, my hand met the dish rack and sent it flying to the floor. The clattering of breaking dishes was a distant echo as the water sloshed around my ears. I felt my lungs giving out, and knew I was only seconds away from inhaling dish-water and drowning. My last thought was that I would be forever known as the girl who drowned in her kitchen sink, then the pressure on the back of my head disappeared.

I reared back out of the water and collapsed to the slippery kitchen tile, sputtering for air as I searched for my attacker. There was no one there, but I could feel energy building in the room, like the feeling right before a storm broke. The kitchen lights began to flicker. At first it was just a few sporadic flashes, then the flickering grew more rapid until the bulbs simultaneously exploded with a starling *pop*. I ducked my head and covered my eyes in shock, then screamed as hands gripped me underneath my armpits and dragged me out of the kitchen.

I struggled, and was just about to burn whoever had me, until the hands let go and I heard Jason's voice as he tried to calm me. I froze, then opened my eyes to look up at him through strands of my dishwater damp hair. He had let go of me to stand a few steps back, likely aware that he'd almost ended up a crispy vampire.

"What happened?" he asked breathlessly as he wiped the water from his hands onto his jeans. His dark blue eyes held concern as he approached and crouched in front of me while I remained huddled on the floor. He took in my wet hair and shirt, then glanced back over his shoulder to the kitchen and the broken dishes all over the floor.

"Something held me under," I wheezed, wrapping my arms around my knees to hold them to my chest. My legs didn't seem to want to work well enough for me to stand.

With a reassuring nod, Jason stood and left me to check the house for intruders. I watched his back, clad in a navy blue tee shirt, as he walked through the living room, then went upstairs. I would have helped him look, but I was still re-learning how to breathe.

He returned a few moments later and crouched in front of me. "There's no one else here. Did you see who it was?"

I shook my head. "They were gone as soon as they let me up, then all of the light bulbs exploded."

Jason offered me a hand and we both stood. Without the hand to support me I would have fallen. Sensing my predicament, he retained his hold on me while he looked back at the kitchen again, deep in thought.

I wrung some of the water out of my hair with my free hand as I looked at him. "Not that I'm not grateful," I began, "but what are you doing here? I mean, I haven't really seen you much since we . . . "

"Broke up," he finished as he turned his gaze back to me.

The words still stung to hear, even though it had been my choice ... mostly.

"Devin asked me to come," he explained.

"Why?" I pressed, beginning to feel more steady.

Jason shook his head as a knock sounded at the door. He looked me up and down. "I'll answer it if you want to get ... cleaned up."

I nodded appreciatively, knowing that I likely had bits of food in my hair from the not very clean dishwater. I let go of his hand, then turned to head toward the stairs. I reached them and ascended quickly, chased off by the sound of Jason opening the front door. I hurried through my bedroom to the the adjoining bathroom, stripping off my damp shirt as I went.

As I stopped to stand in front of the mirror, I observed that I did in fact have food in my hair. I took a shaky breath, feeling almost fearful to turn on the faucet to wash it out.

I looked around the room cautiously, then turned the water on only enough to let out a gentle trickle. With one more glance behind me, I flipped my hair over my head and draped it all into the sink. Once again silently chastising myself for not getting a haircut, I began washing sections of my white-blonde, shoulder blade length hair in the lukewarm water. The process was painfully slow, but I was still too shaken to run the water full-blast.

That done, I did my best at washing my arms, face, and chest in the sink, then grabbed a fluffy purple towel from the rack. I patted my skin dry, then wrapped my hair in the towel as I left the bathroom. Not wanting to waste any more time, I went through my closet, quickly donned a black, long-sleeve tee over my mostly dry jeans, then combed my fingers through my still wet hair. I grabbed the towel where I'd dropped it on the floor and tossed it onto my bed as I left the room, knowing the longer I took, the longer Abel's lecture would be for keeping him waiting.

I left my room and hurried downstairs, actually looking forward to a meeting I had been dreading, solely because after the kitchen experience, I really didn't want to be alone in the house.

I entered the living room to find Jason, Devin, and Abel, seated with two people I didn't know. The first new person was a girl who looked about my age, with dark skin and extremely curly, near-black hair. She looked frail, but in a healthy way, and I could tell that she was probably no more than 5'3", as her feet barely reached the ground from her perch on my cushy loveseat. The other person was older, probably around fifty, and had dusky red hair framing her lightly lined face. She dressed like my mom, kind of conservative hippy, and her serene smile and kind green eyes made me like her instantly.

Abel and Devin both rose from where they sat beside the older woman on the couch to acknowledge me. I didn't see Jason, but I could smell coffee brewing and knew he must be in the kitchen. Better him than me. I wasn't planning on going back into the kitchen ever again, and it wasn't just to avoid doing the dishes.

Abel and Devin both wore suits. Devin looked comfortable, but Abel awkwardly straightened out his slacks as he approached. He was probably wishing he was in his normal attire, a vest with no shirt, or a tight tee shirt. His long, dark hair hanging loose around his striking features was the only hint of casual in his appearance.

"I trust you had a good reason for keeping us waiting?" he questioned as he took in my wet hair with his perceptive, hawk-like eyes.

I smiled sweetly. "You very well know that there's *always* a good reason for everything I do."

Jason entered the room and came to stand beside me with a tray supporting several mugs of coffee. "Someone tried to drown her in the kitchen sink," he explained, looking at Abel.

I gave Jason a sharp look.

"There really isn't a moment's rest with this one," Devin lamented as he ran his fingers through his pale blond hair, mussing its meticulously styled appearance. He winked one of his sky blue eyes at me as I glared at him.

I turned my attention back to Abel. Giving in to the fact that he would want more information, I held up my hands to stop him from speaking. "I didn't see who it was, and the light bulbs mysteriously exploded afterward. That's all I know."

Abel inhaled, then let out a long breath. He gestured back to the two women, who were staring at us like we'd all grown second heads. "Allow me to introduce Emma and Siobhan. I sincerely hope that I haven't brought them into a . . . situation."

He'd gestured to the younger girl as Emma, and the older woman as Siobhan. Both of them looked worried, though Emma much more so than Siobhan. Just judging by appearance, Siobhan didn't strike me as a woman that would get overly worked up by much.

"I'm sure it will be fine," I said patiently as Jason began handing out mugs of coffee. Everyone took one, except for Abel.

Once the coffee was doled out, I helped Jason move two extra chairs from the dining room to the living room so we would all have a place to sit. I ended up in one of the chairs, with Abel in the other, leaving Jason to sit with Devin and Siobhan on the couch. The hierarchy of the seating arrangement was obvious with Abel and I sitting taller than everyone else.

Abel glanced back and forth between my two new pack members. "Do either of you have any questions for Xoe?"

Emma raised her hand sheepishly. After Abel nodded for her to speak, she cleared her throat. "Do you go to high school? I'm supposed to start my senior year in the fall, and I'd really like to graduate."

I cringed. I'd come to terms with remaining a dropout, even though I was living back in the human world. For me, there was just no going back.

"I don't," I replied, not bothering to explain my situation, "but Lucy does. She's another member of the pack, and I'm sure she'd be more than happy to get you settled in."

Emma nodded to herself as Siobhan focused her gaze on me enough to make me uncomfortable. Intelligence radiated from her eyes as she sized me up, then raised her hand to speak.

"What do you expect from your pack members?" she asked before Abel could call on her. I was startled by her southern accent, especially with her Irish name.

I narrowed my eyes at her in confusion. "I'm not quite sure what you mean."

"Well, I've never had a demon Alpha before," she explained. "Do the rest of the pack members still shift together? What are we supposed to do for you?"

I was still confused by her line of questioning. What were they supposed to *do* for me?

"Um," I began, wracking my mind for something to say, "I know Lucy and Max sometimes shift together, so you could probably join them if you want to. Lela tends to keep to herself, and we all try to respect that."

Her eye twitched at the latter part of my explanation, though whether it was the mention of Lela, or that she liked to keep to herself, I wasn't sure.

"And what about my other question?" she replied without missing a beat.

I felt myself blush and I wasn't sure why. Part of me wanted to order her to lay daily offerings at my feet and dance naked in the moonlight, but something told me that Siobhan was not a woman that appreciated being messed with.

"Protect each other?" I said like it was a question.

Siobhan narrowed her eyes, trying to discern whether or not I was being genuine. "You're not like any Alpha I've ever known," she said finally.

I shrugged, not knowing what else to say. The silence began to draw out as we all stared at each other.

"Well," Devin said with a sudden clap of his hands. "I think it's time to get Siobhan and Emma settled into their new home. You can work out your pack . . . dynamics later. The leaders need to have a meeting."

I looked a question at Devin, unaware of any "meeting" besides the awkward one we'd just had. I stood and shook both of the women's hands as they rose, then Devin ushered them out the front door. All three of them left mostly empty mugs of coffee behind. I looked down at my own mug of coffee still clutched in my left hand, then set it down on the coffee table with the others. Coffee and nervous stomach knots simply don't go together.

Abel and Jason had stood with the rest of us, and now returned to their seats. I took one glance at the empty chair beside Abel, then took the empty love seat instead.

"First thing's first," Abel said as he turned to look at Jason. "I have a job for you."

It wasn't the first thing I'd expected to hear, or the middle, or the last, for that matter. Logically, I knew that Abel had hired Jason's services before. Heck, it was how I'd met Jason in the first place, but it seemed like Abel liked having Jason around my little pack. One more scary monster to ward off the bad guys. Would he really choose to send him away now?

My anxious string of thoughts was interrupted as Jason gestured for Abel to continue.

"I was hoping to hire you to watch over Emma," he explained. "She has an abusive father, and I'm worried that he might come looking for her."

"Is her father a werewolf?" Jason asked.

Abel shook his head. "Human, but dangerous."

The thought of Emma with an abusive father gave me chills, and I was suddenly very glad that she had been chosen as one of my new pack members. She seemed so small and helpless. I would just pass off the gratitude that I felt upon learning that Jason wouldn't be chasing some rogue wolf somewhere far away as gratitude that we would get the chance to keep Emma safe. I was grateful for both, but the Jason side of things made me feel weak and pathetic. He wasn't *mine* to keep around.

"Sounds simple enough," Jason replied after a moment of thought.

Abel nodded and handed a piece of paper to Jason. "This is the address of where Emma will be living. I know you'd rather not harm a human, so if he shows up, have Xoe do it."

"Hey!" I exclaimed, taking instant offense at what he'd said. "I'd rather not harm a human either."

Abel grinned at me, and I realized too late that he was pulling my leg. Before I could say something scathing, he asked, "What do you think of your new pack members?"

I shrugged. "They're not what I expected, but they seem nice."

Abel raised a dark brow at me. "What do you mean, *not what you expected*?"

I shrugged again. "Well the whole idea is to make the pack larger and therefore more intimidating. I just assumed that the new wolves themselves would be large and intimidating."

Abel nodded. "I had considered that, but at the end of the day, Emma and Siobhan are more likely to accept a teenage girl as their leader than some of our more formidable wolves."

"Because they're women?" I prompted.

Abel had the grace to look slightly embarrassed. "That, and neither of them are terribly dominant, though Siobhan may pretend to be. It will make for an easy transition, hopefully free of power struggles. There may be men among the next group of new pack members. The only qualification is that they must be less dominant than you."

Jason snorted. "I don't imagine you'll have much

trouble finding plenty of wolves that fit that particular bill."

I turned toward Jason and scowled. "Just what is that supposed to mean?"

He gave me a good-natured smile. "Don't be modest, Xoe. I've never seen you back down to *anyone*."

He'd meant the words in a joking way, but I could sense some bitterness behind them. We had, after all, broken up because of that very personality trait.

I took a deep breath and let the line of questioning go. "So where will they live? Is Emma even old enough to be on her own?"

"Siobhan is Emma's guardian," Abel explained. "Emma's father lost custody when her mother died. He's an addict with multiple convictions. Siobhan has been a foster parent for many years, and she's helped to raise many young wolves left without parents, so it was only natural that Emma go to her."

"But her dad has refused to leave the picture entirely?" I prompted.

Abel answered with a curt nod. "We've done our best to keep him away thus far, but he has eluded our grasp."

I laughed bitterly. "I imagine the *grasp* to which you are referring would come with some very sharp claws."

Abel nodded again, this time with a secretive smile.

I smirked. "Is this whole foster parent thing even legal?" I asked skeptically, mainly because I wasn't sure how Abel would have otherwise managed to make sure that wolf children didn't end up with human foster parents.

Abel chuckled to himself. "Emma was placed with Siobhan by the state of California, and the state also permitted their move to Oregon." When I raised an eyebrow at him, he added, "You're not the only one with friends in high places."

I squinted at him. As far as I was aware, *he* was the only one with friends in high places. "I don't follow," I admitted.

"Well, you have *me*," he explained, "and word on the street is that many of the upper demons are beginning to take an interest in you."

My mood instantly soured. "The last two upper demons that took an interest in me are dead. Three, if you include my father."

Abel bit his lip, and judging by his expression, if he was a little more flexible he would have lifted his foot into his mouth. "I didn't mean to bring up any hurtful subjects," he said evenly.

I shrugged and shelved the pain of my father's death and my grandmother's betrayal to the back of my mind, where it had been resting and gathering dust for the past several weeks.

"Okay," I sighed after a moment. "I assume we've gone over everything? I'll introduce Emma and Siobhan to the others, and Jason will make sure that Emma's dad doesn't come near her?"

"That's correct," Abel stated as he stood. "Devin and I

will wait in town for another week or so, just to make sure we don't have any more . . . mishaps. Then you will be on your own."

"Peachy," I replied, actually not looking forward to things getting back to normal. At least with the constant drama, I didn't have to deal with being a jobless, fatherless, high-school drop out.

Abel shook Jason's hand as Jason stood, and I stood and offered my hand as well. At first I thought Abel was going to snub me, but then he leaned in and pulled me into an uncomfortable hug.

"I truly am sorry about your father," he said softly as he patted my back lightly.

A moment later, the embrace was over and he headed for the door without another word. I scrunched my eyebrows at Jason in confusion.

He shrugged in reply as Abel shut the door behind him.

Jason and I had a moment of awkward silence before he said, "I suppose I should go find Emma, but . . . "

"But . . . " I pressed.

Jason sighed. "I know it's not my place, but I'd rather you not be alone after what happened in the kitchen."

My heart sped a little at the recent memory. Honestly, I didn't want to be alone either, but I couldn't ask Jason to stay with me. I had somewhere to be. "I promised Dorrie I'd visit today, so I won't be alone. Maybe I'll go to the demon library and look up invisible beasties that try to drown people in dirty dishwater."

"You can just tell me you're going to see Chase," Jason stated bluntly.

My mouth dropped at his accusation. Sure, I *was* planning on seeing Chase, but I really had promised Dorrie a visit.

"He's still looking for Sam," I replied, "and I can poof us around the underground much faster than Chase can run." Okay, maybe I was making up excuses. True excuses, but excuses none-the-less.

"I really don't think he believed your grandmother would hurt either of you," Jason said sadly. "Maybe you should just let him go."

I felt a wash of anger, but forced it back down. "He may not have believed it, but he still tricked us. That trick cost my father his life. Sam will pay for that, if nothing else."

Jason shook his head. "Okay, I'm sorry for bringing anything up. It really isn't my place."

"You're entitled to your own opinions," I assured, though the scowl I felt on my face probably didn't help to back up my words.

Jason put his hands in his pockets and gave me a long, searching look. I wasn't sure what he found, but with another sigh he announced, "I'll go find Emma. Let me know when you're ready to introduce her to Lucy and the others."

I nodded. In the blink of an eye, Jason was gone, and the door was shut and locked behind him. I took a few steps forward and glanced into the kitchen to find Jason had cleaned up the water and broken dishes while I was in the shower. The light bulbs had been replaced as well, and there wasn't a hint of glass from their explosions. What I wouldn't give to be able to clean with supernatural speed and multitasking abilities.

I looked at the clock to see that I still had a good five hours before my mom would get home from work. I wasn't sure if whatever had attacked me would go after her, but better safe than sorry. My visit to the underground would have to be a short one. Dorrie would be disappointed. Chase probably would too . . . so would I, but don't tell anyone. It will be our little secret.

Made in the USA
San Bernardino, CA
28 January 2020